happiness

and the Lithuanian Countess

*Sofija and Vladimir Zubov with their son Vladimir,
about 1890.*

happiness

and the Lithuanian Countess

Sofia Zubov
Jolanta Kriuniene
Ruta Sevo

First Printing: February 2017
ISBN 978-0-9905862-3-4 paperback
ISBN 978-0-9905862-4-1 ebook (Kindle)

Momox Publishing
Contact: ruta@momox.org
www.momox.org

Available as a paperback or an ebook, online
Cover design: Ruta Sevo
HAPPINESS was originally published in 1902 in Polish.

The Lithuanian translation of the novel, *Laimė*, was
published in April, 2015 by Verba Vera, Kaunas, Lithuania.
Available at https://www.knygos.lt/lt/knygos/laime/

For the kin who escaped after WW II and thrived in America but lost a deep connection to their heritage, and for my great-grandmother Sofija whose intellectual life was foiled
-Ruta Sevo

The publishers [of Laimė, the Lithuanian translation from Polish] are truly grateful to Mrs. Dalia Palukaitienė for permission to publish the novel, providing photographs from the family archive, and assistance in preparing the press release for the translation.
-Jolanta Kriūnienė

TABLE OF CONTENTS

Happiness by Sofia Zubov

PREFACE

Count Vladimir and Countess Sofija Zubov are the grandparents of Vladimir Zubov who married Danutė Čiurlionytė, the daughter of Mikalojaus Konstantinas Čiurlionas.

They enter the history of Lithuania as philanthropists and leaders in society. They founded and supported Lithuanian-language schools, distributed Lithuanian newspapers during the time when the Lithuanian press was banned, promoted festivals on their estate—secret gatherings of leading lights of Lithuania, organized a public library society, financed the creation of a higher school for girls in Šiauliai, and promoted economic development through their own model research farms. Sadly, happiness within their own family deteriorated: after twenty-six years of a shared life, the couple separated.

The novel "Laimė" [happiness] was issued in 1902, well before it could garner any meaningful feedback from a wide public. Sofija Bilevičiūtė-Zubovienė's husband, after reading autobiographical elements that permeate the story, bought up and destroyed the whole print run. One copy survived to this day in the library of a Čiurlionis' granddaughter, Dalia Palukaitienė.

Why did Count Zubov do this? A mystery of one hundred years unfolds, when you read the pages of this unique work.

- Jolanta Kriūnienė

HAPPINESS

Sofia Zubov

Retreat[1]

A heat wave was making everybody in Warsaw miserable. Mr. Mykolas Sokolskis decided to retreat to the countryside. All of his friends and family had already left town. They'd invited him to visit their country houses, but the thought held him back: he'd find himself with the same people who bored him all winter. If not for the heat, Mr. Mykolas would've stayed in town through the whole summer.

He was a thirty-three-year-old man about town and quite rich. From time to time he wrote articles for newspapers, and that's why people called him a writer. He needed a change of venue, an escape from his mother's persistent matchmaking and the polite atmosphere of pretense in which he was forced to circulate. He decided to take a trip to Lithuania and visit his old friend Steponas Orvidas, a friend from university days who'd kindly invited him.

When the train puffed into the station where a carriage was supposed to meet him, he was overcome with a joy he hadn't felt since childhood. He felt invigorated. Steponas was there to meet him. Their reunion – simple, heartfelt, with no

---

[1] The original novel had no chapter titles. These were added because they are required in ebooks and seem more interesting than numbers. Per RS.

pretense – was really pleasant. He felt quite at ease and so absorbed riding in the carriage with his old friend that he didn't even notice when they pulled up to the veranda in front of the house.

"Tea is being served on the veranda," a butler told him, as he helped him shake off the dust of the journey and wash his hands.

"I'll introduce you to the family," Steponas said, taking Mykolas by the arm and leading him to the veranda. The guest first greeted the lady of the manor, then her mother, then the teacher and finally children, of which there were four: three boys and one girl.

There was a time when Mykolas liked to flirt when he was in Warsaw, but in recent years it was just a habit, just as it was a habit to associate with tiresome and boring people. He had a knack for figuring women out: he could guess from barely one look how he could charm them. He knew how to flirt with whom from an early age, if he felt the slightest impulse to start this form of entertainment.

He didn't usually invite single ladies to a flirting contest. He was afraid his mother would feel the need to appeal to his sense of decency and demand that this sport end with him being led to the altar. Therefore, he flirted with engaged ladies and was very selective, because a long chase ruined the fun. Up to a year now he'd gotten even more selective and laid back. Women seemed especially dull, weak and without principles: it was enough to mock them or call them old-fashioned and superstitious. The minute he dismissed them they chased him like a prophet through fire and ice.

Here and now, Mykolas, with his special talent, got a look at Mrs. Steponiene. Judging by the age of her children, she was at least thirty-five years old, but she didn't look even thirty. She was pretty, though slightly plump, with a graceful figure; a smiling, sweet face framed in slightly curly dark hair; gazing out with big, dewy blue eyes; white skin highlighted by rosy cheeks. Her features were, to be honest, not outstanding, but expressed youth and health.

They looked eye to eye. Mrs. Steponiene gazed at him with a quiet scrutiny, as if he weren't a living man but a statue. All of a sudden, she smiled.

"I see, Sir, that you're taken aback that I'm looking you over like this. I want to form a first impression of you, and then later, when I get to know you better, confirm whether I was right, and demonstrate how much we women can tell about a person from his appearance."

Although she smiled as she spoke, Mykolas, with all his insight, saw not a hint of flirtation. She smiled the same way as she spoke politely with her mother, the teacher and the children. She looked at her husband and talked to him with another expression. This expression masked a greater sincerity, but at the same time, some kind of sadness or heartache. Mykolas was unable to figure out the authentic self behind her expression. Her face was both proud and resigned at the same time.

"I hope you'll be spending the whole summer with us," said Steponas. "I warn you at the outset, the only people who feel good in the country are those who like to be free and on their own. I can't stand it when you stay with people and the hosts don't take even one step away. That's why my wife and I don't look after our guests. Maybe we don't give them enough attention, but we all have our own lives. For guests who don't like to be left to themselves too much, we're glad to spend some of our free time with them."

3

After he said that, Steponas stood up from the table, went over to Mykolas, slapped him on the shoulder, smiled amiably and offered to show him to the room prepared for him.

Mykolas bowed to the hostess and followed Steponas. His room was upstairs, with a balcony overlooking the garden.

"On this balcony, you're both in the house and in the garden, right? I won't take you on a tour of the farm today because you're probably tired. I'll be back in a few hours."

Steponas left.

Mr. Mykolas carried an arm chair out onto the balcony and was truly happy that he was left alone quickly and without ceremony, in such a cozy little room.

Voices in the Garden

Soon it got dark. Everything was quiet after a sultry day.

Not one branch moved. A dog barked in the distance. Nearby, a warbler trilled in the bush.

"Vytukai! Maryte!" He heard Mrs. Steponiene's voice in the garden.

Darn it, Mr. Mykolas thought. *The kids are going to ruin my perfect mood tonight.* Then he heard children moving about. The little ones were running along the path to their mother.

"Hush! Quiet!" she told them. She sat on a bench not far from the balcony, facing the children. "Kids, listen closely to this special night. It's rare. We need to pay attention, because to experience a minute like this means we've earned one more moment of happiness in life. I'm sure that today, every beetle, every ant is appreciating this quiet, warm air!"

"Mama, is today a good day for everyone in the world? Everyone?" asked Maryte, eight years old.

Mykolas heard how Mrs. Steponiene sighed.

"Oh no! Everyone can't be happy too. But everyone who's healthy, calm, free and without a care – they're as delighted as we are in this moment of happiness."

"Mama, why just a moment?" asked one of the boys.

Philosopher, thought Mr. Mykolas and listened without a word because he was interested in the answer.

"I told you over and over, kids," pausing to think a bit, "that everybody who is alive in the world wants to be alive

5

and has to want to be alive – like you, for example, have to sleep on the ground, although you might want to just soar above it. Well now, try jumping up…"

The kids jumped up and about, laughing, delighted with the impossibility of flying.

Mrs. Steponiene continued,

"You see, now? Since you have to sleep on the ground, you have to want to live there…. Only sick or very unhappy people think: 'Why do I stay alive? My life is miserable. I'd rather be dead.' And believe me, a person who is tormented that much often decides to die and is fooling himself, that he doesn't want to live any more. And what if, around that time, some evil criminal attacks him. You would think that this miserable person is going to be happy that a bad guy wants to kill him. But not at all! You can be sure he'll start shouting for help, defend himself or run frantically from death. That's because, for him and for every living being, there's an instinct to live… Anyway, the dew's falling. It's time to go in the house, kids. I'll finish talking in the house."

Mrs. Steponiene and her brood disappeared.

I'm not happy, thought Mr. Mykolas. *She started an entire lecture on the instinct to survive, and I don't see how that relates to the little nugget about happiness in the world. Very interesting. Maybe I didn't get what she was trying to say?"* Frustrated, he asked himself whether the little talk could possibly settle the question. *It seems she was trying to explain why there's little happiness in the world? What would I say if somebody asked me?* Suddenly he burst out laughing. *What's the point of straining your brain! The question's as crazy as asking why a fly has four legs instead of six.*

However, his confidence in this judgement didn't last. He thought about the example of the instinct to live, and got worried again. Eventually he decided to tell Mrs. Steponiene that he'd accidently overheard her talk with the children and ask her to explain the question. His train of thought was interrupted by a knock on the door and the voice of Steponas.

"My wife says to invite you to dinner. We don't usually eat dinner, just a light tea. We're making an exception. Do you take dinner?"

"My friend, don't forget I'm a city person. We don't eat a lot. After such a filling and truly country-style afternoon-tea today, I can't possibly eat another bite."

"Then tell my wife yourself," grumbled Steponas, and, taking Mykolas by the arm, led him downstairs to the same veranda where they just had tea.

As he kissed Mrs. Steponiene's hand, Mykolas apologized for causing her any inconvenience.

"Mama, why didn't you ask Mr. Mykolas first, if he wanted to have dinner?" said Maryte.

"Because, child, I don't know Mr. Mykolas well enough to know if he's going to be honest about what he'd like. Anyway, why the rush to ask? We can ask later. You're going to annoy our guest with needless questions. It's not a problem."

Maryte blushed and hung her head, as Mykolas tried to ease her embarrassment with a hug.

"Since you're going to let me stay in the country such a long time, I hope you won't treat me like a guest before whom the children must be careful. I ask Madam to let Maryte ask away freely, anything she wants to ask."

Mrs. Elvyra smiled.

"Thank you, Sir," she answered. "I've encouraged her to ask questions, because there's no greater joy than to teach my precious minds to learn about life. I only worry about one

7

thing: that my guests will lose patience, because I never miss an opportunity to explain things to my children. Really, are you bothered by their questions? Please be honest."

She looked at Mykolas frankly and deferentially after she spoke. His conventional self knew that he had to be prepared to be honest or else she would think him insincere.

"Let's just say, a *la longue*[2] the endless 'why?' can be tedious. On the other hand, Madam's answers are interesting. I assure you that they can be very instructive to me also."

Mrs. Steponiene told him not to be silly.

"Mama, is it true that Christ reached the very top of the tower?" asked the oldest boy, Jasius.

"Yes, son. Nobody climbed higher."

"May I ask, what tower are you referring to?" asked Mykolas.

"Well, you see, Sir," Mrs. Steponiene answered, a little out of sorts, "Today we had a geography lesson and I told them that the higher we climb, the wider our horizon. Whenever possible I relate their study of nature to real life or morality. Today I compared a geographic horizon with a moral outlook. It seems to me," she blushed a bit, "that evil and egotism rise from erroneous ways of thinking about life. Christ outdid all of us through the ages, and that's why we can't reach His level."

"It seems you take the phrase 'way of thinking' to a wider sense. In the example you just presented, a 'wide perspective' is an orientation to existence. It's not an approach to the every-day and the mundane, to the conditions that are firmly grounded in the pages of history.

---

[2] French, "in the long run"

Am I to understand that you're calling morality a way of life? Short and sweet. Might I ask you to explain this idea of yours further?"

Just then the clock chimed ten o'clock. Mrs. Steponiene looked at the children and asked Mykolas to excuse her to put the children to bed. She graciously and sincerely asked him not to be offended, in a way that made him seem an old friend.

"I'll happily explain my thinking to you," she said leaving, "I just beg you to be patient."

"Would you like a cigar?" asked Steponas, coming in, who'd been called away briefly on some business.

"No thanks, I don't smoke. Besides, it'd be a shame to spoil your wonderful country air with smoke."

They were both silent for a while.

"Your wife. She's a philosopher," Mykolas was the first to speak.

"You figured that out? You know, her philosophizing bothers me, especially because she pushes it on the kids. It could turn them into oddballs!"

"But the kids make a very good impression, and there's nothing in your wife's talk that's apparently irrational. On the contrary, I'm impressed with the simplicity and clarity of her views."

"I think Elvyra's an exceptional woman, too," said Steponas, with an expression of manly pride, hearing praise for his wife. "But she was raised differently and now she doesn't grasp all the things her education gave her. Everything is fundamentally realized through the laws of nature, which are expressed as an instinct for self-preservation, for both the person and the species. She's created an entire ethic that she's trying to apply to child rearing."

Just then Elvyra returned.

"I see that Steponas is taking over in explaining my views. I'm amazed, because he isn't really interested in them. He's worried that I might harm the kids and inoculate them against his own values. I can't convince him, although we're both basically in agreement, that the most important thing in raising children is to instill good habits. You see, good behavior can discourage some wrong ideas. After all, habit is second nature."

"I could argue with you about some of your assumptions, but I have to go and finish writing a letter." Steponas looked at Mykolas and said, "After Elvyra explains it to you, her *idee fixe*, you and I can discuss it."

He made this disparaging comment in a tone that disarmed the wounding irony.

After he left, Mykolas turned to Elvyra and asked her for the explanation she'd promised. Elvyra could see that he was interested. Feeling somewhat pleased with herself and afraid of disappointing her guest if she ignored his curiosity, she began explaining with eyes glowing, while Mykolas every now and then interrupted with his questions.

"I have to warn you at the outset, I have no intention of making up something new. I just want to say that in general we don't pay enough attention to things that are familiar to us. We do a poor job of hearing what animate nature tells us, and, too often, we allow imagined fantasies to take over."

As she talked with renewed animation, her cheeks flushed pink again and she was breathing faster. While Mykolas listened attentively and with real interest, he couldn't help but notice what an attractive philosopher she was.

"I know, Sir, you may be thinking, 'How can you be sure that you're capable of intuiting what nature is telling us?' To which I answer, that on the contrary, I don't claim that I have the best understanding or feeling, actually, when I spell out the reasoning that leads me to shape my theory, I think it'll be clear. In raising my children – by the way, my own beliefs in this regard are neutral – I wasn't able to instill in them fear of a higher power nor a hope for rewards in the afterlife. Still, I feel it's essential to teach the children how to behave among those close to them, every step of the way.

"I asked myself: do you want your children to be righteous, unselfish, intelligent, and so on? Why don't you ultimately put this in the hands of God, and don't be afraid of Hell? What's your answer, Sir?" she asked, charming in her excitement.

"I don't have any kids," said Mr. Mykolas. "I've never thought about it, but I suppose it's a bad thing for them to be angry or selfish."

"I'm happy to hear that you think along the same lines as I do, because I find it hard to talk to people who insist on saying that selfish values are good and that the selfish are happier than the good. I think you can only feel blessed if you feel happiness inside, surrounded by others who are also happy and can look you straight in the eye. A career doesn't bring you the privilege of that kind of happiness. That's why altruism is the expression of a good, thoughtful education. I think that you, Sir, also assign this meaning to the words 'upbringing' or 'worldview.'"

It was obvious that the meeting of their views was assuring, because she spoke more calmly and with confidence after that.

"As you can see, Sir, I'd answer the question as follows, and I've studied it myself: If you thought it was most important to break with conventions, then maybe it really would be better to be selfish, false, and so on. Eventually I decided: it bothers me that society, of which I am a part, moves along just fine. I decided that it pains me that there is a lot of evil in it—even though my life from the very first peep has seen none of that. It also makes me glad that I'm becoming someone who ensures the well-being of the society, although from my perspective it should require real sacrifices.

"What's the basis for my identity with the core of society?" she asked herself, here remembering a quotation from Weismann[3]: "'Nature cares about the species, not the individual.' Hegel understood this, when he claimed once that the species or family is more real than the individual. Humans are a tiny part of the animal kingdom, and therein as part of nature, get stronger or develop as a species and are preserved or evolve. If we observe a couple of parents (human or animal), who refuse to eat food in order to save the lives of their offspring, isn't that a law of nature, that the entire organic world obeys instinctively? When we see buffaloes fighting to defend their herd, isn't that the same? And the plants in the world: when they sprout in a place where they're doomed to die off in a drought, they quicken

---

[3] August Weismann (1834–1914) – a German biologist and theoretician about evolution.

their maturation, in order to scatter their seeds before they die. Do we need more examples?"

She fell silent for a minute, and something troubled her lovely face.

"By the way, I don't know how to tell you my thoughts in a clear order, one following from the other. If you aren't bored yet, I'll keep talking and explain a few things that are essential if you want to understand my theory."

Mykolas assured her that he would be confused if she didn't explain further. He convinced Elvyra with just one look that it wasn't just an empty compliment and she'd no reason to fear that his words were insincere.

She smiled and continued:

"Have you Sir, ever asked yourself, what it means to be happy?"

Charmed by her playful expression, Mykolas considered answering the compliment saying: "Happiness – hearing that and seeing such an attractive philosopher like you" or something like that. But he sensed that it would be inappropriate.

Still, he had to reply somehow.

"Happiness? Happiness – to have most of your needs met," he threw out a hackneyed phrase.

"Ah, you don't always have happiness when you have what you said. I won't contradict your opinion, but I'll just tell you what it seems to me. Happiness – that's an interior state of mind that comes of winning the struggle for survival – your own, and the existence of everyone else."

"How do you mean?" Mykolas sounded surprised. "You can't be happy otherwise?"

"There's nothing without it," she answered firmly. "If you look closely at the lives of other people, you'll see that everything is exclusively and especially about the struggle for survival, not every day, but in the broad sense of the word. For example, when you eat, you certainly are in a struggle for survival, for your very being, and trying to win the fight because for the time being you are safe from dying of starvation. When we get dressed, we dress to keep from freezing.

"I'm sure that our thoughts and everything that we're used to calling spiritual power is nothing but a manifestation of the instinct for survival. In human beings, who are struggling for survival along with the rest of all living creatures in the world, this instinct is expressed in a far more complex fashion. The mind, the will, love and so forth – these are all tools for survival.

"The moment of triumph for the instinct is the moment of happiness and joy, that we have succeeded in living in a way that our particular nature requires. Joy is witness to the fact that even though we're physically and spiritually separate individuals, we firmly hold fast to the struggle to survive in the world, with the promise that we'll live better in the future. Maybe that's why our blessings are always like lights, flashing and unreachable in the distance. I hope, while you're visiting with us, you come across many examples that support what I'm talking about in general. But is that what you're interested in?" she asked looking Mykolas directly in the eye.

Mykolas assured her that he listened attentively and quietly only in order to hear every word of her interesting conclusions.

"It's not good that you aren't arguing," she said, "Because if you disagreed, it would be easier for me to explain, rather than to talk through everything by myself.

You could, for example, doubt the assumptions behind my definition of 'happiness,' citing the fact that not only among people but also among other creatures, there are occasionally cases of devotion to their genus or nest, in a word, based on facts, that contradict the instinct of the survival.

"But that's deceptive... Those examples just substantiate Wiessman' point of view that nature primarily tries to preserve not separate individuals, but the species. So, having examined this instinct, I came to the conclusion that what we call the instinct for survival is nothing but the instinct for the survival of selective species. According to Wiessman, the life span of an individual is the result of adaptation and the life is as long as it is necessary for the species. That means the majority of male insects live only until they secure the reproduction of their own species. The same way, the individual will to live is like the instinct for the survival of the species, as we say, 'The individual lives for the species.'

"The interests of the species are suppressed in humans, who are endowed with a developed spirituality. The most complex life-form cries out in the fight for ideas, for the existence of itself and all people. Different epochs are marked by various struggles, according to their models, organization, and beliefs. We think about our spiritual legacies, so to speak, innumerable times more than we worry about our direct physical descendants.

"In truth, there is only one instinct, one natural goal in the organic world: the survival of the species. Everything else is either a phase of the instinct, or an expression of it."

It seemed to Mykolas that Elvyra paused for a moment and put her hand to her forehead in order to summon a thought. "I'm impressed with your system. I don't want to interrupt." She smiled and her eyes expressed gratitude although a little frown of concentration passed over her brow.

"Of course!" Her eyes blazed again. "Without being aware of it ourselves, we're driven by this instinct, sort of an instrument in somebody else's hands for some unknown purpose: the strange, mysterious side of our existence. It's really amazing that the well-being of an individual being is quite closely bound to the needs of the species. I have to bring your attention to the various stages of the evolution of a species in which we see every step, among humans and among living creatures. For example, we know the difference between males who force themselves on a female but then don't bother themselves with the progeny (like rabbits), and males who take care of their progeny with the female partner.

"And look here, for species of the highest order, the instinct for preservation is but a brief moment of reproduction, a natural instinct, or simply altruism. Whereas for species of the lowest order, the same instinct for survival—wherein the individual tries to save its species, to take care of itself—that we call that instinct for self-preservation egoism. Isn't that right?" she asked. "Consider, Sir, how we're to interpret those statements. If I'm sure that you've understood my thinking, it won't be important whether they're right or whether science defines them another way."

Mykolas summarized her point, to be sure that he'd understood it, and then listened further.

"Well, let's return to the example of the males. In the first, altruism doesn't seem to be developed. In the second, altruism is strong, because he's suppressing his egotism to devote himself to tending to the young. I'm not talking about a complex form of altruism, unique to humans. For a minute,

16

let's look at these two cases with regard to well-being. The first father is happy because he's satisfied his instinct for survival, that is to say, he himself is healthy, fulfilled, and satisfying his instinct for the survival of his species in the simplest way: he finds a mate. He'll be happy and content even in a situation where his children die of hunger beside him, because some higher instinct for survival has no meaning for him – he is not driven by it. He has food to eat, he has company, and nothing else is important! That means he's won the struggle for survival, because he's found the necessities of life and found a mate.

"The second male, having the same situation, is not happy, because his predominant instinct is to strive higher and it incorporates a wish for descendants who are his very own. For him to be happy he needs, on top of everything the first one settles for, is to see to the welfare of his progeny. If they aren't taken care of, then there isn't a harmony between his aspirations and their happiness, not to mention their well-being. In humans, it's even more complicated by the fact that our predominant instinct is spiritual, and we think about our descendants far down the road, caring for the whole nation. We want to see it prosperous and happy.

"For individuals in whom this type of instinct is highly developed, there is no well-being without ideas. It isn't just important to directly satisfy the instinct for physical survival, it's also important that their future spiritual descendants are also happy. That broader life philosophy, which is often unconscious, creates for them the greatest moments of deep satisfaction.

"When our individual needs and fulfillment connect, reach a point of high contentment, I call it the magical side of life. It just strengthens your subtle soul. I've had little time to read lately. It could be that what I'm saying is already common knowledge and maybe even put into practice.

"I'm beyond grateful to you, Sir, that you've heard me out with such respect. Honestly, it's the first time in my life. Usually people accuse me of not making sense the minute I open my mouth, or they complain right away and don't try to understand."

Steponas came in, interrupting her,

"Enough with the philosophy, people. Did you realize it's one o'clock already? Elvyra, you probably forgot that you've got to go to Smiltishkes early tomorrow, to see to the first milking operation?"

"Oh, Steponas, dear, it's all right if I'm a little short on sleep. I'll go in any case. Did you remember to ask that the horses be ready?"

"Horses will be ready," Steponas muttered with anger. "It seems to me it doesn't make sense to go without a good night's sleep. You'll be tired and won't take care of things."

Wishing Mykolas good-night, Elvyra gave him a friendly hand-shake and thanked him again for the thoughtful conversation. Steponas gave his wife a dirty look, suggesting to her that Mykolas only listened to be polite and that he would have rather preferred to rest after journey.

Mykolas had trouble falling asleep. Here was something that caught his interest, lifted him from the malaise he'd sunk into for several years. "What's taken hold of me here?" he asked himself, out of a habit of analyzing his thoughts and feelings. The conversation replayed in his mind, raising a lot of questions. He had a strong impulse to pose them to Elvyra and hear the answers.

From the very first days, he intuited, rather than understood, that his arguments wouldn't undermine her theories, which she'd thought a lot about and never had to defend. And what difference did it make if she were kind enough to share the details of her worldview?

He put out the light. His mind was restless. Although he was tired, there was no hope for sleep. He closed his eyes. The face of Elvyra appeared even more vibrant. It seemed to him he could hear her sweet voice, and it just animated her face even more.

"Hells bells," he said to himself. "Is this love at first sight, like a foolish boy? Me, an extinct volcano?"

He pondered the crazy idea out loud. After a while, fatigue took over and a veil of dreams cloaked his mind. Mykolas dreamed of himself in this home where he'd been received so warmly, with such affection, as if he were a fine, honorable gentleman. It was good for his soul, as if he'd returned home from a foreign land.

Horse Trading

Early in the morning he was wakened to hear the clatter of a wagon and the snap of reins. It was past ten a.m., he noticed, and he leaped from bed as if bitten. He dressed quickly and went out onto the veranda. A maid worked alone. She carried dishes on a tray, a setting for one person. For him, she explained, the guest sleeping in.

"What shall I pour for you, Sir? Coffee? Tea?" Elvyra's mother asked as she sat down beside the coffee pot, directing him to a seat.

Mrs. Songailiene stopped him as he tried to explain and apologize for sleeping in so long.

"It's just fine! Didn't you come to the country to relax, Sir? The charm of the country makes you free. My son-in-law and daughter will never make you jump out of bed early. In any case, what would you do with yourself in the early morning? They usually make the rounds of the farm first thing in the morning. My daughter then spends some time on lessons with her son. He has exams after the vacation. You wouldn't have much fun spending time with old me. And Mr. Vytautas, the tutor, spends mornings on his own studies and Latin language lessons with our Jasius."

Steponas led a newly arrived guest to the veranda. Introductions were made. This was the guest whose noisy wagon had wakened Mykolas. Anupras Zodeika, a close neighbor of Steponas and Elvyra. He began to chat about the economy, about the fact that there were few farmers and workers, because they had emigrated *en mass* to America, about low prices for crops. In a word, they talked about problems totally foreign to Mykolas. Eventually, Mr. Anupras Zodeika changed the subject, addressing Steponas.

"You know, I rode over with the horses your wife wanted to trade for a few of your Dereshas[4] horses. Do you want go look them over?"

"Sure," said Steponas, "But let's wait for Elvyra. We just returned from Smiltishkes and she went to change."

That's where she went, Mykolas thought to himself, feeling happy that he would see her soon. *Honestly, really, have I taken an interest so fast?* he asked himself and in the same minute rejected the idea, explaining to himself that it wasn't strange that he wanted the friendship of this woman. She was the most interesting person here.

Elvyra came in – glowing with health, not a hint that she lacked sleep, flushing from the heat of the trip back from the Smiltishkes farm. The rosy cheeks went well with her dark curly hair and a modest batiste[5] dress in solid heliotrope. She greeted everyone as if she were among old friends, which behavior seemed quite congenial to Mykolas. He'd been bored during his host's small talk, and now he suddenly felt completely at home and comfortable.

Everyone gathered in the stables. Steponas, like a true horse breeder and expert, started to look over Zodeika's horses with a practiced eye. He measured them and asked for them to be walked back and forth on harness. He stated his opinion: the legs were too short, hooves in good shape,

---

[4] Dereshas – brown and white haired horse
[5] Plain weave cotton

haunches a little weak, and so on. Mykolas, who had never visited a farm, loved the horses. Some seemed really nice, and others, lame, but he really had no sense for what were good and bad qualities.

"So, Elvyra, do you want to buy the horses?" Steponas asked. "The breed isn't a suitable one, but if you really like them, we can keep a few."

"No. I really don't want them. They don't fit our stable, and we don't need them. I wouldn't want you to buy them just to please me, without any real need," she said with some intensity.

Meanwhile on Steponas' request, the horses were queued up to be shown.

Mykolas sidled over to Elvyra and said that, clearly, she loved horses and knew a lot about them.

"I can't claim to know a lot. I'm around experts like Steponas, Anupras and various other people who come by every day, sometimes twice a day, to look over horses. Whether I want to or not, I've learned a lot about them – what are good features, what are bad ones. We've been standing here nearly a whole hour. It would take me a whole week for this kind of inspection, but look, Sir, how Steponas and Anupras just jump right in, and love every minute."

"That's for sure," said Mykolas, watching the two men, who'd already looked over the horses ten times, ask for them to be ushered out again, in order to appraise their plusses and minuses all over again.

Elvyra asked, "I'd be interested to know how would you rate this group of horses?"

Mykolas confessed honestly that he wasn't competent in this area.

"Do you perceive a competition here?"

"I have to confess that I don't understand what you're talking about."

"About what? Well, usually, a dramatic competition crops up. Each of them wants to have the best reputation in the horse market, that's why each of them has to compare his animal with the nearest competitor. You want to stand out among horse breeders, more or less a consistent reputation. You have to rate your horses and others constantly, because there's no more volatile market than this. But most amazing to me is that they themselves don't suspect: they're inspired not by their love of horses, but their love of competition."

"In other words, you think these two are more caught up in the idea of making money? I say 'making money' because, it seems to me, these two men aren't in a situation that requires them to compete aggressively."

"Who knows if either of them even has a special passion to make a profit per se. But doesn't it seem to you, Sir, that we fight not only because of obvious needs? Some sports are just fun, and we get better at them when we do them. Like one of the oldest sports – wrestling, that even animals do, trying to develop their strength."

A servant appeared, distracting them from watching the horses, and invited them to dinner.

"Steponas, dear, please, take everybody to dinner now because the dumplings will get cold!"

Mykolas accompanied Elvyra, thinking the others would follow behind. When they went into the dining room, they found Mrs. Songailiene, Mr. Vytautas and the children there.

"Steponas is incorrigible," said Mrs. Songailiene. "He's never on time."

It was clear that Steponas' cavalier ways were quite annoying to his mother-in-law. Older people especially are upset to have their meal delayed. That's why Elvyra calmed her mother down with a very sweet look, showing not the slightest impatience.

"It's not a problem, Mama. I had Steponas' dumplings put aside to cook later, and we'll go ahead and eat." Having said that, she sat down next to her mother, and steered Mykonas to the place next to her.

When the servant appeared in door to the dining room with a bowl full of dumplings, the kids jumped up and down in their chairs, squirming with joy, yelling all together: "Dumplings! Oh boy, dumplings!"

"Mama, why don't we have dumplings more often?" Maryte asked outright. "When I grow up, I'm going to have dumplings every day!" she added with enthusiasm.

"I'd like to see if you felt the same way after eating them three days in a row," Elvyra said, laughing. "Would you have the same taste for dumplings that you have for bread, which we eat every day? Why don't you jump for joy when you see bread?"

"Because bread is nothing special to me, Mama. It doesn't taste good or bad." Maryte said, explaining her opinion. "If you didn't give us bread very often, it wouldn't bother me. I wouldn't be disappointed."

"Mama, let's not give Maryte bread for a week, then, and see if she misses it," exclaimed the oldest boy Jasius.

"You think I'll miss it? Not a bit!" Maryte blustered back, wanting to defend to her proclamation to her brother. "All right, Mama. Don't give me bread for a week. We'll see if I miss it."

"All right, Maryte," her mother answered. "You can try it. It's better if you convince yourself. I've seen many poor people who have nothing to eat except a few pieces of black bread. Once I saw somebody slice his bread very thin and as he raised it to his mouth, he looked at it ravenously, as if it were a great delicacy. I understood," she looked over at Mykolas, "that to a person who has a terrible hunger, a morsel of bread saves him from starving to death, and eating it is truly a victory, making him very happy. Here we sit at the table always half full and, rather than mainly restoring our bodies, we fill our bellies, and from that excess we get all kinds of health problems. In effect, we undo our own happiness!" continued Elvyra, with even more fervor. "Sir, surely you're aware of the Weber's physiological law: the tension of pressure will grow in an arithmetic progression, while the stimulus or excitement should increase geometrically."

Mykolas did not know this law. He saw no reason to hide his ignorance, because, truth be told, until then he'd had little interest in physiology or psychology. Completely without hesitation he asked her to explain.

"It's even more interesting," explained Elvyra, "as a first principle in the science of psychology. It's not hard to understand, given that that particular science gives us the basis for such various and complex inquiries, that Weber took it a great leap forward when he understood that in reality our feeling of dependence on others is a unique constant. Just recall, Sir, various thoughts and pleasures and you'll find it the same everywhere – stated another way, our happiness and memories depend on the degree of excitement.

"Besides, who doesn't know that if you experience something over a long time, then it doesn't reach our subconscious, and we feel as if the thing didn't exist. It's even more important to understand, to comprehend this principle, and we'll find happiness more easily, avoiding all kinds of harm, especially if it's experienced too often."

Finally, Steponas returned with Anupras, and in a few minutes, dumplings appeared on the table. Anupras blamed his host for being late.

"Oh, no need to apologize. We didn't wait for you and we took care of our pressing hunger. After that we lost track of time, talking."

Having said that, Elvyra looked over at Mykolas with a seeming question.

She asked him under her breath, "Are you honestly not laughing at me for claiming that we lost track of time, when I was the only one talking you to death, possibly being a terrible bore?"

"My goodness, Madam!" Mykolas answered in the same whisper. "How can I convince you that I enjoyed every word? You may not believe me when I tell you, from my heart, that I don't remember a more pleasant conversation in my life."

Elvyra, giving him the sweetest look, said,

"I believe you, and I'm glad." Her face was glowing again.

In the very next minute she assumed the role of hostess, checking to see if the guests needed anything. Seeing a bit of impatience in Mrs. Songailiene's face, she summoned the servant with a nod of her head and asked that the rest of the meal be brought as soon as possible. She assessed what everyone needed and took care of it, pleasantly taking part in the general conversation.

As they got up from the table, they heard the clatter of a wagon. Steponas went out first to greet the guests. In a few minutes, he came back and spoke to his wife.

"Come quick. Mrs. Bzezinska and Mrs. Dauksiene arrived. They're waiting for you in the parlor."

Anupras quickly stood up and excused himself to the hosts and the other guests, saying he promised his wife he would come home early.

"If you can't stay, well, go on," grumbled Steponas, not making an effort to keep him.

Steponas saw Anupras out to the foyer and came back to the dining room. Although Mykolas wanted to escape into the garden, Steponas persuaded him to go visit with the ladies, asking him to help entertain them on his behalf.

Both ladies were young and elegant. They came to invite the Orvidas to a charity event they were organizing, and they asked Elvyra to accept the role of hostess for the dinner.

"And Sir, are you going to stay at Egliai very long?" asked Bzezinska, sending a coquettish expression in his direction.

"If the Orvidas don't throw me out, I'd like to stay the whole summer." He answered, with a nod toward Elvyra.

"We'll throw you out. Surely, we will," she joked.

Bzezinska, beside herself with glee that she might have a new dance partner, and they were rare, took it on herself to pressure Mykolas to come to the event.

"You have such kind eyes. Surely, you're a philanthropist. It wouldn't be proper to miss this party."

Mykolas thanked her for the invitation and objected to the characterization.

"I don't approve of a charity that promises to solve poverty. Also, it's a drop in the ocean to provide a little help to a few unfortunate people when a hundred thousand are dying somewhere, of hunger and disease. A charity is more a pleasure for its naive advocates than it is useful to the poor. Besides, it encourages the proliferation of beggars and networks of crooks. I'm not saying I won't help when I see there's a real benefit for the poor, but I do it from purely selfish motives, because the sight of suffering is very distressing."

The gathering was taken by surprise by Mykolas' rather unusual perspective. Elvyra listened closely. It was obvious that she was impatiently waiting for him to finish.

"Well said, Sir!" She said enthusiastically, as soon as he was silent. "I never thought, given our short acquaintance, that you could suppress your conscience so well. All the good and bad done in society is reflected in our hearts, because the individual is society in microcosm. I see, Sir, the idea is buried deep inside you, and you feel it."

Mykolas wanted to protest, but Elvyra interrupted and asked,

"I beg you, beg you, Sir, please listen while I finish. When I'm done, I'll listen to you with respect."

Mykolas politely conceded.

"If we want to position ourselves as best as possible in the struggles of life, we don't have to avoid reality. On the contrary, we want to try to know it well. You, Sir, are asserting that when you see poverty up close you refuse to help because it's distressing to see others suffer. But why is that sight so distressing? Because, in your mind, Sir, humanity is dying because of this suffering, and that's what suffering does, and we want to save mankind from its demise.

"And that's not all. If you, Sir, won't help people who are suffering and dying, and let misfortune persist, then that uncomfortable feeling that everybody calls shame will hound you everywhere. That feeling confirms that we experience not only benefits or harms to our person, but also the benefits and harms done to society. In a word, this is the working of the instinct for the survival of the species.

"You assert that good deeds enable beggars and cheats. But that's not true! For the most part, we can say that goodness often benefits not those who are in material need, but those who are moral beggars. Still people continue to be poor, because they are very badly armed in the struggle for the survival. Unless they have a great need, and then they'll humiliate themselves, scrounge and exploit the resources of their relatives. But beggars like that are not made because of charity! As long as society fails to feed and shine a light on every one of its members, we've had and will have unfortunate people, regardless of good works."

Elvyra went quiet. Her face showed a weariness and a frustration that she wasn't able to explain the point in her mind as well as she wanted to, that she failed to be as clear as she wanted.

Mykolas looked at her with genuine respect. During the short time he'd been in Egliai, she came across as wonderfully different: wise, when she was expressing her ideas; childlike, when she blushed; heated, when she was angry with him for putting down philanthropy.

That's an amazing woman here, indeed, he thought. He considered that if he admitted he was wrong, he might get more attention. He said:

"I have to agree that the honorable Lady is right. For myself, let me beat my chest and admit that I'm wrong about these issues due to my sleeping conscience."

He spoke in his usual laid-back manner. Steponas rightly sensed a shadow of irony, but Elvyra, gullible and good-hearted by nature, didn't in the least question Mykolas' words. Her eyes glistened with righteousness.

Steponas was quiet through the whole exchange. His face showed his impatience.

Seeing that, Elvyra stopped talking, her spirit deflated. Seeing the brow of the head of the household, she sensed that he was getting tired from the guests. Shortly after that, the guests said their good-byes and left. But Steponas continued to sit, in a sullen mood. Suddenly he had the urge to ride to one of the farthest farms. He asked for horses to be saddled and went to his office, and then a few minutes later summoned his wife.

Mykolas was left alone in the dining room. Various thoughts buzzed in his head like a hornet's nest. He wanted to line them up somehow and recover his balance. He went out into the garden. The heat had lifted. Finally, a soothing air flowed through the shady garden. A wind was pleasantly refreshing. He walked around the garden.

The house and garden were on plateau high above Venta. Below, a river flowed through the foothills, cutting deeply. One side was steep and abrupt, and the other, the opposite, a little lower, sandy, overgrown with vegetation. It was possible to take winding paths down through trees and brush to the river. There was a little hut for changing clothes where the trail ended, and even closer floated a boat tied near a bridge.

Vytautas was resting in the boat, waiting, according to him, for the children. They were supposed to come down with Elvyra in order to cross the river and go walking in the pine forest. Vytautas held a book in his hands. He was obviously preoccupied and answered Mykolas' questions in a cool tone. The latter, not understanding the reason for this coldness, decided he was an unwelcome visitor and climbed back up the hill on the same path.

He met Elvyra and the children along the row of plum trees. Maryte held two ropes in her hands, ostensibly reins, and waved them to urge on Vytukas and Adomelis, who were jumping around like unruly horses. After them came Elvyra, with her arm around Jasius' shoulders as he hugged her. Her face was still as serious as it was when she left the parlor. She looked as if she were troubled and something was eating at her heart.

Sensing her mood, Mykolas didn't dare ask to come along, even though he felt like telling her his thoughts and ask her a thousand questions that were still stirring since yesterday.

Elvyra spoke first and asked:

"Maybe you'd like to come on the river with us and go walking in the forest?"

"If it's no bother. I'd love to keep you company," he said.

"I'm not sure if I can trust you with one of my little schemes," Elvyra said, pausing on the path and drawing something in the sand. "Mr. Vytautas is an ardent Lithuanian: he believes that Lithuania will yet have its own literature, which it hasn't had until now, and that the language will find a rightful place in contemporary literature. I don't believe in this dream, but still, I sympathize with a

32

belief that encourages people to work together and explore ideas which I'm sure will serve society one way or another.

"Although I shared my opinion with Vytautas quite openly, I wasn't able to convince him. Quite the opposite. I see in him a fierce determination to draw me over to his side. I've been eager to read Lithuanian literature for a long time now, but something always gets in my way. That's why I wanted to listen to him read today when we walk with the kids, like we do every day. And that's why, you see," she spoke with some concern, "I don't know if Vytautas is going to want to read to us and if you won't be bored listening to a language you don't know."

Now Mykolas understood Vytautas' aloofness. Still, he told Elvyra that although he wanted to finish the conversation they'd started as soon as possible and tell her a few observations about her views, he could be patient and wait until the reading was over and Jasius came back in the boat.

"Are you bothered by my being candid?" Elvyra asked, now in a better mood and with a happy and sincere expression.

"I'm only glad you can be open," Mykolas assured her.

Elvyra and her gaggle of children, who were now restless from being held back, went down the path to the river, and Mykolas stayed in the garden.

Beautiful lanes of old lindens extended on both sides of the garden, making so much shade that the ground under their boughs was wet while elsewhere the earth was parched from the sun. Rays of sunlight heavily saturated lower bushes, and light patterns on the black path shimmered only when the wind stirred the tops of the linden trees. Benches stood here and there.

Mykolas sat down on one and lost himself in thought.

The instinct for survival is the foundation for the meaning of all life, he thought. *She managed to explain a wide range of behaviors and many so-called spiritual rules, about things such as mind, memory, imagination and et cetera. She calls them instruments of the instinct for self-preservation or its manifestation. Even so, she failed to explain the essence of our own souls – souls that imply that we have everlasting life, which itself is confirmed in the proposition: 'I think, therefore I am.'*

He couldn't sit still, restless. He jumped up and paced the walkways, then sat down again on a bench, eager to speak to Elvyra as soon as possible.

Let her theory explain what is feeling, he repeated to himself, delighted that he'd found a flaw in her whole system. He expected to be right, and he was overcome with a smug satisfaction that he hadn't felt in a long time. He brashly asked himself, *And what's going to make me happier than winning an argument with her?*

This notion rather darkened his self-satisfaction, as if a new weight had been put on the other side of the scale.

Sure, maybe her concept of happiness is right, he thought, sitting down again. *But … her theory fails to explain the soul or feelings of human beings. Sure. Everything she says only applies to a limited type of reality in which the soul is already aligned with conscious thought. However, she doesn't explain the instinct in the finest sense, that is the unconscious soul, or the universal soul, the soul which is as infinite as the universe.*

His self-confidence came back.

She called morality a 'philosophy of life.' It turns out that we can only be happy when we are, in spite of ourselves, working for the benefit of humanity. In other words, we need to steadily rise above our personal disagreements, above class struggle and racial conflict and unite into one human race, and then, as a united force, conquer the biological world, take control over nature, the whole globe. Start to figure out our place in the whole world – that's a goal of humanity. Yes, the theory is nice, he reflected. Respect for Elvyra filtered through the line of his thought.

At the end of the lane, Jasius appeared. He ran toward him and shouted:

"Mr. Mykolas, I was looking for you!"

Mykolas quickly rushed to the breathless boy, worried that there'd been a boating accident. Jasius assured him: nothing like that. Elvyra herself came along with him, but then rushed off to prepare the evening meal for the children, while Jasius, who'd eaten, needed to row a boat to the opposite shore right away, because the children were waiting there with Vytautas. As soon as he came back, they were all going to go to a "desert island," which was to the right of the pine forest.

"It's a real island," chattered Jasius. "You need to take a boat out there with us some time, Sir. You'd see what a great house we're building! You don't know that we're like Robinson Crusoe, the Swiss man. My name is Henrikas, and right now I've returned to the shipwreck to get food from storage. We've put together a house with things we could salvage from the shipwreck. Mama's going to give us a basket of sandwiches, soup and water, and then I'll take it back."

He couldn't stop talking about Robinson, but Mykolas interrupted:

"Is your mother going out to the desert island too?"

"No. She's not going this time, because she wants to talk to you."

"Did she tell you that?" Mykolas' interest peaked.

"She told Mr. Vytautas," answered Jasius and, hearing his mother calling, ran home.

Mykolas turned after him. Just then he saw Elvyra helping Jasius carry a basket. They went toward the river. He rushed to take the basket from her hands, and, although the others protested, he carried it to the bridge and put it in the boat.

"Mama, remember the big turtle that pulled our boat? I think Mr. Mykolas is like that turtle, and that's why we asked him to help, right, Mama?" Jasius asked.

"Okay, okay. But be careful and sit in the very middle of the boat so you don't fall in the water," the mother warned, and watched her son row away until he reached the opposite shore.

"Now let's go for a walk or go back to the house. Which do you prefer, Sir? I was afraid that we wouldn't be able to talk easily with my son asking for something every minute. I'm anxious to hear your analysis!"

Mikolas said he wanted to stay in the garden. He sat down on a bench under a large oak beside the river. It had a clear view of anything going on at the desert island.

"You wouldn't believe how the children love that island," said Elvyra. "It tests their skills. They learn to solve various problems, and everything they find can be used to build or set up the house. They spend all day, morning until night, without our attention. That's why, I'm telling you, everything they find gives them such a great thrill. They've planted beds of peas, radishes, and potatoes for themselves. They'll realize their dream when they finish the house. I'm sure that vegetables they've grown themselves will taste much better than the various good foods they get without effort. I'm delighted to hear their ideas, because that kind of play builds character, instills in them a sense of harmony, respect for each other's needs and wants. In other words, it's like a microcosm of the world, in which at their age it's typical for imagination to override reality. Like Jasius turning you into a turtle," she added laughing.

Mykolas didn't know the world of children at all. That's why he tried to steer the conversation in another direction.

"If I may, I'd like to ask you a few questions, related to our prior conversations."

"I'm listening," she said, with the same slight blush as the evening before.

"You maintain that the instinct for survival is the alpha and omega of everything. Please explain to me the role that feelings serve in that," he began, laying the groundwork for the argument he'd prepared.

He spoke with full confidence in himself.

"I don't understand what you're trying to get at," she answered with surprise. "Is it possible you have ten mysteries instead of only one? There's only one mystery for me: 'life!'"

"And what do you call the soul in this schema? The soul that feels that it's an infinite expression, that's able to reassert its existence, as every one of us experiences for himself, and whose instrument is the brain?" he spoke, somewhat riled and worried that his reasoning would be put down. A feeling that the woman's hand would hurt his pride.

Elvyra sensed that.

"Mykolas, it seems to me that we've both taken a wrong turn. There was no need for me to ask you if you have ten mysteries instead of one. I can see that you're somewhat put off that I went deeper into these things, as a woman. Yes, it's true that I'm a little more carried away by this than you, because life has pushed me there. You, Sir, are single, and I have a family. For that reason alone, I had to explain to myself something that is totally unimportant to you, Sir. In raising children, I had to rack my brains over a number of questions, because they're essential and the food of morality. That's why, I think, you shouldn't take offense that I'm more primed to have a philosophy of life.

"For example, you're not offended that Steponas knows more about horses than you do. A person can't do everything. That's why there's a division of labor in society: some try to understand the meaning of life, others work to improve some aspect of it. Do you mean to say that you don't acknowledge the importance of people like naturalists who spend their whole life dedicated to researching single-celled *infusoria*? Obviously, the attempt to seek knowledge, sooner or later, will inform a broader philosophical discourse about existence, foresee dangers and forestall them."

Mykolas listened to her pleasant voice and let his aggressive impulse go. Elvyra had an extraordinary ability to excite a listener's interest. If Mykolas hadn't until then completely accepted her theory, now he was completely convinced.

"You're absolutely right," he said. "I have to admit that I've never met a woman like you in my life. ... Maybe you don't believe me, and take it as flattery?"

He looked her directly in the eye and – what a shock! – felt at the same time shy and a great joy, a feeling that came over him a long time ago, when he felt his heart leap for the first time in the presence of a woman.

He was nineteen years old at the time. It was evening, then. His beloved was dancing, euphoric with the idea of freedom, and asked with feigned sincerity during the cotillion, "Tell me, Sir, which would you sacrifice, the individual to society or society to the individual?" Staring at her beauty, her deep black eyes, he answered: "Society to the individual!" and with his look, suggested "Of course, the same as you." All the while continuing to stare, he saw that she understood, and at once he worried that he'd said too much, but he was also glad that he'd decided to engage her. But it turned out that she didn't know how to read him. She took offense, angry at his joke, and attacked him: "Then you, Sir, you put your selfishness in first place?! Well, perfect! I have no words! I never imagined that a man could be so blunt and confess!"

Here and now looking at Elvyra, he got the same feeling that he'd said too much and that she'd read his eyes and assumed that he'd fallen in love with her, a stranger's wife. And he was dismayed, that just like selfishness back then, now the seeming deceit of a friend would trigger angry words. He was shaken that he would lose a chance to be friends with her… But nothing like that happened, because the woman before him was not a naïve teenager, but a temperate, tactful and wise woman. Truth be told, she flushed at his words (she said herself it was a weak spot), but, looking him in the eye, she calmly and simply answered:

"In general, I believe that you might not have met a woman like me. Certainly, you've met others instead. But seriously, I think," she repeated in earnest, "that maybe you never came across a woman who was a non-believer and yet had a clear purpose in life, that is to say, believed in a path to achieve happiness. You've not met one, Sir, because that type of person is just now emerging. I just realized barely three years ago, what my soul felt for a long time already. If you haven't met women like that, my intuition tells me, it's because you haven't tried to see them up close. Aren't there women like that, for example, Anele Kromicka?"

"Anele?!" sputtered Mykolas.

"Do you remember, where it's said, 'You can claim anything, but when you do something wrong, your conscience always says: Wrong! Wrong, and you won't convince anyone!' But I digress. It means that you want to hear what I think about the soul." She leaned back lightly against the oak tree, while her whole thin figure was bowed toward him.

No unseemly feelings woke in him – dishonorable, exciting – as her pale forehead was close to him, with the breeze fluttering dark curly hair above it. Her skinny arm was close, braced on the small bench. For the first time in his life he didn't respond to the womanly side of a woman. She was like a fortune-teller whose every word evoked in him the soul of an innocent, those days when he knew how to feel alive and craved heat when he knew what was pleasure and what was really pain.

Only two days ago, it seemed to him that nothing could move him, surprise or grab him. Lonely days went by, full of doubt, tedious and meaningless. He was tired of people he hung out with and the norms of high society that he couldn't escape. In other words, he lived out of habit and conformity. And here this enchantress changed him in just the first night: he felt as if something in him woke from a long sleep. And here today he sees that an awareness has come to life that was dormant, an awareness of human connection, an awareness like nerves linking him with missing puzzle pieces to one organism: humanity. Yes, those nerves had been dead in him, or maybe severed from the organism of humanity, because he only felt suffering that befell him personally, and he didn't feel the suffering of society.

Now, looking at her, he felt the fresh feeling of his heart flooding with joy. It was different from what he experienced loving tempting, desirable women. He listened to Elvyra with rapt attention, as she tried to instill in him her worldly secrets.

"According to that principle," she said, "it means that everything that's alive wants to live and wants to preserve its species. Every creature fights for those two birthrights and struggles, because life calls many to the feast but selects only a few to stay. There are billions of those who want to live and only a small percentage of those who can. Every living creature tries its best to win the struggle to survive. That 'aspiration' is fierce and strong in the plant and animal kingdoms, and in humanity, and we submit to it equally. It's like the force of gravity that we can't escape.

"There are two things all living creatures share, everywhere: evolution and the fight for life. Probably, they may both be an expression of the same aspiration, but I'm not talking about that now. Both of these elements already appear in the simplest single-celled organisms. The cell lives, helped by endosmosis and exosmosis, interacting to stimuli in its environment, struggling to exist. If it didn't grow, it would exhaust the elements it needs to sustain life. By growing, it's saved from death, evolving to a new and unexplored state.

"In other words, growth is a driving force in the struggle for survival, its mechanism.

"After this we have the mystery of life unfold and such an infinite profusion of branches flourish that it's hard to comprehend the continuous proliferation of new derivatives and directions. At least I finally see clearly, that diversification is synonymous with mystery we call 'life.' Adaptation to environmental conditions and heredity are like two big branches of the same tree. After all, isn't it wonderful that the entire expression of an individual is contained in a tiny embryo, the full complexity of traits accrued through the ages in the fight for survival?

"I'd like to draw your attention to the fact that in the march toward diversity and adaptation to new paths and conditions, the world of living creatures has separated itself out in giving humans dominion over the soul, namely: will, intelligence, memory, imagination, and etc. It's nothing but self-preservation or the expression of the instinct to survive. As I said, it's the same instinct, just at different stages of development.

"Human life is the trunk of a tree, crowned with the richest coronet of branches and twigs. It ultimately blooms in a triumph over our personalities and consciousness."

"You've been able to describe your view of the world in most poetic terms," said Mykolas. "Just let me ask, please, what's the basis for your premise that our personality is shaped by adaptation in the evolutionary struggle for survival?"

"I don't tie it exclusively to blooming trees. By no means. The same life force and feeling that pulses in very single-celled organism is stronger and more specialized in complex organisms, that have ever more complex nervous systems. The same life force and feeling culminates its development in the achievement of human intelligence, and is expressed in personality.

"That means our personality is not separate from the domain of our soul – memory, imagination, intelligence, will and other expressions of our instinct for survival. Rather, they're parts of the whole. Or, vice versa: these parts of ourselves together comprise our personality, and each of them is indeed integral to the others, that it's impossible to imagine 'an independent memory' or 'an independent idea.' For example, suppose we want to imagine something. We have to draw on our memory, because no one's managed to imagine something that's never been seen apart from its association with a thing. Absolutely no one, anyone not even the most impoverished soul!

"Enough philosophy?" They heard a bold, playful voice. It was Steponas, who'd returned from riding, and was surprised to find Elvyra and Mykolas still in the dining room after dinner.

"Elvyra, why are you bothering Mykolas with your 'struggle for survival?' You'll see, he's going to tear out of here. It's such a nice day, and you're sitting inside! It's a shame."

"We just came back from a walk," said Elvyra and cheerfully told her husband about the children's trip to the island and how they'd made up wild, imaginary adventures.

The three moved to the veranda for tea, where others had already settled in.

About ten p.m., Elvyra went to put the children to bed as usual. Songailiene, worried about the evening humidity, excused herself. Vytautas went off to work in his room. Steponas asked Mykolas,

"Tell me, Mykolas, honestly, don't you think Elvyra's a joke with all that philosophy?"

"A joke?!" Mykolas protested heatedly. "What are talking about, Steponas? I respect her as a highly unusual woman. Her enthusiasm surprises me, and her intensity is charming. Her questions just confirm the wisdom of the proverb: 'You won't be superior in your own country.'"

Steponas shrugged.

"I mean, you and our neighbors look at Elvyra as if she were obsessed with an *idée fixe*, and it even seemed to me that you were talking to her with a little irony. I admit I didn't like it. I went out riding without inviting you because I didn't want you to see me in a bad mood."

It was clear that Mykolas' respect for his wife made Steponas happy.

In a Mirror

Elvyra, before going to bed, hugged every sleeping child and kissed each lightly on the brow. She whispered with bliss: "My special treasure!"

After that she promptly took off her dress, put on a white nightgown, and sat in front of a mirror. She raised a hand to take a clip from her hair and looked at her reflection. Her arms came out of a sleeve with a stitched pattern and an arc of light seemed to surround her head. Her face was beautiful, framed in loose, buoyant, curly, dark hair. A hint of a satisfied smile passed Elvyra's lips and lingered in her eyes.

If all of 'them,' she said, thinking about men who'd admired her, *could see me like this, I wouldn't feel that it's a secret that I'm attractive. Here Steponas sees me every day without having to make any effort, and he doesn't notice what I'm wearing, how I look. Like a watchmaker who can't hear his own clock's alarm.*

She sighed, ran her fingers through her hair, and leaned on her elbows lost in thought. She reflected on her whole life; she pictured herself as a young, beautiful woman. She reflected on Steponas – how he was back when they fell in love: full of energy, devoted to her, and fascinated by her. In those days, he noticed everything: her inside, her outside, everything about her was precious, even sublime to him. She remembered how Steponas kissed the white scarf around her neck, just because it was her scarf! How happy they were then! A lot of time had passed, a lot of things changed between them, and those changes gave her pause.

Elvyra came from a family that had been wealthy and then ruined, materially speaking. She had a very levelheaded mother who couldn't stand people who put on airs. She raised her children to work and to do chores. To her children, Songailiene possibly painted life in colors that were too dark. She lectured that nothing in life is free. "You want to be good, you want to be helpful to others, and not only because people rarely get their fair reward, but because a lack of good character is immediately obvious. It's like the clothing we wear: very often people don't notice what you're wearing but if your clothes are a mess, they see it immediately." Another point of wisdom instilled in children by Songailiene: "Don't be sad, but rather be glad that people will judge you more harshly than others. If people expect more of you, in other words, they'll also hold you in higher esteem. When we expect little of someone, we also don't value them as much."

Elvyra, as the oldest daughter, shared her parents' worry and aspirations about raising seven children on a low budget, to feed and clothe all of them. They worked hard to accomplish what they hoped for. The whole family pulled together toward this common goal, and as it is often in a shared effort, they had high focus and energy. Every member of the family knew how hard they worked and had great respect for work, to save time and money and to give up unnecessary things. The difference in age between the oldest and youngest children was twenty years. When Elvyra became engaged, the job of raising all seven children was still by no means finished. That's why, even though she was in love and blessed with good fortune, she felt that Steponas had pulled her away from a duty that wasn't finished. She continued to feel a great loyalty to the nest in which she'd grown up, and because of that she was very nurturing to her own home fire.

Elvyra had a good education and tried very hard to instill a deep feeling of harmony in her own family. To her it was a connection to the experience of society, her values – a value for the human race. She was bothered by anything that strained those connections, and delighted by anything that preserved and bolstered them. Trying to understand these feelings made her stronger in the struggle for harmony in her own nest. Elvyra loved her husband, and she was his beloved great treasure. She greatly valued her husband's kindness, his sensitivity to the misfortunes of others, his nobility, energy, diligence, finally his solid posture, and his looks, which expressed spiritual goodness.

Unfortunately, her sensitive nature picked up that Steponas slowly started to treat her as if she were a possession, a piece of property that you don't have to look after. Before, he cherished her above everything else and now he would lash out with surprising criticism and at times showed people close to him that she was appreciated much less. She saw how Steponas was sweet and congenial in the company of strangers, but when the two were alone, he was sullen and got mean over little things. It was a great strain on her and she couldn't figure out why he'd changed.

She closely observed relationships between other spouses, and unfortunately, with rare exception the same thing happened everywhere she looked. Especially in prominent aristocratic families. The husbands surprisingly quickly started to feel like they owned their wives and showed them no respect. In some cases, they even succumbed to abuse and broke their marital vows. Harmony and peace continued most often when the man and woman pulled together, solving common problems in life and raising children as a team. In those cases, each valued the help of the other, and in dealing with worries about children they didn't let some incident disturb the cohesion of the family.

For sure, there were exceptions even among wealthy couples. The reason was either a deep faith on the part of the wife, or, a mending of fences (in this case positive) when the man, for example, was at fault and he was from a modest and poor family, and saw his own marriage as a tremendous wonderful opportunity. He appreciated his wife and wanted to be an asset to her. In that kind of family, harmony and mutual trust prevail, especially when the wife is good, devoted to her children and appreciative of her husband.

But what happened between me and Steponas? she asked herself more than once. Steponas by nature wasn't frivolous and loved children. He'd always championed democratic ideas, which suggested that the differences between them due to economic status couldn't be behind the negative change. However, when she realized that Steponas had, from time to time, started to seek the company of "flirting" women, she didn't sense or grasp at first that something threatened their family hearth. It wasn't easy to find an answer: how to behave, what to do, what to work on. She felt intuitively that it wouldn't work to confront her husband. She understood – while Steponas was married and he hadn't technically broken his vows, there was no way he would understand her psyche. On the contrary, he'd jump to berate her, blame her, and then claim that he, by his very nature, can't stand conflict and criticism, that his behavior is honest and above suspicion and that he'll always do whatever he wants.

She remembered a similar quarrel with Steponas one time, when she stood up to his domineering mother over some misbehavior and decided to make fun of her "old-fashioned ideas." Hearing his wife's whispered comment, Steponas reacted with anger, charging that she wasn't what she used to be, that her ideas were changing, and theory was the most important thing to her in her search for the truth, yet she herself condemned it and pointed a finger at his sincerity. He said he'd long thought they were entirely different people and that she was trying to provoke him, looking for things that made them different instead of talking about what they had in common.

Elvyra was stunned. Her heart broke so bad she couldn't say a word. Nothing like it had happened before. The earth froze under her feet. It seemed to her that this exchange ended everything, that there was no other way except to separate from her husband. What was left was to decide about the children.

Having poured out his bile and stopped talking, Steponas saw her devastation. He was astonished at her silence. Wanting to appear calm and now reserved, he said:

"You talk about truth all the time and think you're perfect. But you're wrong about me. I say exactly what I think. Whereas you do your best to hide. I tell you completely straight: I love my freedom and will never let anyone take it from me. Will not!" he shouted. "Even if it means separating from you. Will not!" he barked again. "And don't think you'll be able to break me!"

Elvyra felt like she was going to faint. She took hold of a chair. She stared at him stupefied, not believing her eyes, her ears, that he, whose welfare was all she ever worried about. She, who as much as possible accommodated his

49

wishes and never pressured him. He, Steponas, whom she at one time loved without end, was horribly brutal to her now. At the moment, they were in the bedroom. Checking on Maryte's little bed, she roused herself and thought, she needed to pull herself together for the sake of the children.

"Steponas," she said quietly, "I'm not going to bother answering your complaints, because that won't get us anywhere. I get, very clearly, that you're mad at me, and that we have to separate. It's sad." Tears choked her voice. "That... that... we're parting in such an awful way."

"What?! Since when are we separating?!.. I wasn't even thinking that." Steponas roared, with rage and irony. "But if you prefer that, I'm not going to beg for mercy. Let me tell you straight: never for a second did I regret that I married you, and I know I couldn't find a better wife. If you want to divorce over a few reckless words, it's clear that you're not happy with me. I won't hang on, and, if you want, I can leave today."

"Steponas," Elvyra interrupted, her handkerchief dabbing tears from her eyes, "Please. Remember our agreement before we got married? We promised each other that we'll be honest. We'll live together in freedom, without anger, right up until we feel that it's bad between us. Steponas, let's be true to that promise!"

"Aren't we true to that promise?" Steponas said in anger. "Am I keeping you? Please don't try to put the blame on me, because you're to blame too: how many dramatic scenes and how many hideous tears have poured from your eyes, even though you know I can't stand them," he stated emphasizing every word.

Overwhelmed by his new grievances, feeling morally crushed that her husband not only did not want to understand her, but he even seemed to mock her love. Elvyra wiped her eyes, straightened up, and, trying to remain calm, said:

"Can you hear me out without interrupting me?"

"Okay," mumbled Steponas and proceeded to pace around the room.

"I've known for a long time now," Elvyra began, "that I annoy you. I don't know how to roll over, and I don't want to 'break' myself. All my efforts to make you happy with me seem to have failed. That's why I think we need to separate. It wouldn't be hard, except for the children. It's not only about us, but about them that we need to talk."

"You mean to say that I don't mean anything to you now?" Steponas said, for the first time in a calm tone, looking at his wife with intensity. "Of course, if your great concern for my welfare is over, and you want to forget me, I don't ask for your charity. Do what you want!"

"But tell me, Steponas," Elvyra turned to him. "Do you still want me as a wife? You haven't even been nice to me in a long time. You treat me as if I were a burden you can't get rid of with any decency."

Tears filled Elvyra's eyes again. She wanted to leave the room and hide from her husband because it hurt to be mocked as if without mercy. But Steponas kept her.

"Please. Don't leave. We need to decide something."

"I'm too upset. I can't stop crying." Elvyra stammered, turning back to her husband.

"Well, then, don't hold back. This is important! I got angry and made a mistake! And, you're quite able to see a lot of things wrong with me, things I say by accident, but when I say something nice, you don't hear it. You don't get it: you only hear bad things. And you lash right back! Don't you feel that I love you and appreciate you, and that I've never thought about getting divorced? What to do! In fact, I'm not going to change. Accept me as I am and I'm at your service. If you can't accept me, I won't beg."

He spoke in a tone that meant he wanted to reconcile. Elvyra, whom he'd accused of not understanding him, sensed right away that he wanted to appease her and not allow the family to be torn apart.

"I see," she said, "that even though you're often angry, you don't want to lose me. I assure you, Steponas, that without good reason and a strong conviction, I won't leave and destroy our home, solely because of the children."

"And I," said Steponas, kissing his wife's tearful eyes, "wouldn't leave, even if we didn't have children, because I love you in spite of any philosophy, just for yourself. I complain because I love you. If I didn't care about you, I'd pretend to be agreeable just like people in many marriages where the husband and wife have nothing in common and their union is in name only."

In front of a mirror, a thoughtful Elvyra vividly remembered their first disagreement, and many after that one. Now she felt utterly helpless, having no one to comfort her, advise her, tell her troubles, or even just show her sympathy. She didn't want to talk to her mother for comfort. She went for a walk confused and depressed, wanting to avoid thinking about it, even avoiding any social contact.

A time came when she saw a real improvement in Steponas' behavior toward her. He became sensitive and attentive. She was not too excited about this change because she suspected that his tenderness was some kind of compensation for an offense that she didn't know about. Life became intolerable and difficult for her.

Her self-esteem and her pride were insulted every time she had to show him affection. She knew that he loved her in an odd way, but he sought the company of other women even more often, because their infatuation with him made him confident that he would have them sooner or later. Elvyra wasn't suspicious, because she wouldn't humble herself to compete with them. It hurt that her husband, her Steponas, who was precious, the father of her children, could forget about them to have fun and indulge in superficial flirtations. He seemed like a man who hid his riches afraid that the devil will come and take them. In the same way someone might not care which crook robbed him, the same way Elvyra didn't care if another woman played a part in her husbands' moral downfall. It mainly hurt that her own treasure wasn't well-hidden and the devil could get to it.

Songailiene, with a woman's intuition, saw her daughter's pain and anxiety and guessed the reason for it, but she was much too tactful and smart to try to discuss it with her daughter. Even so, once, seeing her very unhappy and brooding, she hugged her poor daughter and said,

"My dear, I see that something's bothering you. Let me tell you advice that's saved me from troubles in my life. I found this piece of wisdom in the book 'Seeking Christ:' 'If you don't know what to do, do what you would in the best of circumstances.'"

The advice worked. It inspired Elvyra and helped her decide how to deal with her husband going forward.

"I'm going to treat him as if he were the best," she said, "While there are things that aren't clear, and while my doubts aren't confirmed by specific facts. That way I can get my balance back, which I need while I raise children."

Heeding this advice, Elvyra was able to work more and her communication with her husband became more harmonious and stable. She never spied on her husband. But earlier she had a dark thought: she didn't really want to admit to herself that she suspected him. Now it was clear that she needed to wait until the truth revealed itself and that it was wrong to darken with suspicion herself, her children, and her husband's life. After that she didn't question what to do in certain situations to find out why Steponas, the Steponas she used to idealize, changed overnight, but tried to find a way to convince him he was behaving badly.

She thought about this problem. She read about it in various books, in which she sought answers to her troubling questions. She talked with various people. All of it led Elvyra a little toward the conclusion that, in her times, married life was one of the most frequent source of unhappiness in the world. She understood that marital happiness, which at the beginning is grounded in physical pleasure, at first brings fulfillment, but then it turns into habit and then even abuse. It is said that not one lady of the manor could sleep, from the beginning of landowners and serfs, until the maid had tickled her feet. Is it strange that the same thing still happens?

Nevertheless, it's a feature of lower organisms that they squander all their vital energy in breeding, not having any other supports in the struggle for survival. This is the only way they can try to preserve their species. A human, the same way, who uses up too much energy in breeding, pandering to the instinct to reproduce, relinquishes a stronger position in which he has thousands of other ways to preserve his species. That kind of person demotes himself to the level of the lowest organism, that squanders its energy in reproduction.

It was clear to Elvyra after that, why neither men nor women become more passionate at a mature age, say forty years old, than they were in adolescence, even though by nature every organism senses a very strong call to preserve the species. It became clear why degenerates were always parasites: a lazy man, incapable of fulfilling the goal of human enlightenment for lack of motivation, becomes interested in various other ways of preserving the species, but not the most important – reproduction.

It became clear that when Steponas fell in love with her, he was motivated to engage the struggle for survival and unconsciously sought a mother for his children – a mother as strong, healthy, beautiful, educated and intelligent, strong-willed and like-minded as his own. In those days, he looked down on women who flirted with him, because he saw that they had capricious feelings and confused minds, although he didn't understand that very well. He felt that the struggle for his own future was stronger than they were. He felt that he didn't have to resort to deception in these matters like they did, and dishonesty was always a pathetic quality.

Now she saw how this same Steponas' moral strength was slowly running down, how he was pandering to his desire more often, ever more often talking cynically and declaring that monogamy in these times wasn't normal and that we have to strive for the ideal – free love.

Elvyra was tormented when she heard this kind of talk around innocent children. It wasn't only bad for their self-esteem, but it sanctioned promiscuity and lechery toward young people. After all, they could take in Steponas' talk and gradually turn their lives to a selfish appetite for flirting.

Steponas had been an only child, spoiled by his mother and everyone around him. They were wealthy, which meant all his whims were indulged. In truth, his innate sense of integrity and generosity won over negative qualities for the most part. When he studied at the university, he was actively engaged in social causes, defending the weak with compassion. He was a member of groups that were progressive in their thinking. They were hardened by misery, resilient in face of life's hardships, and were disgusted with any kind of transgression—and transgression for them included the use of prostitutes.

That's the man Elvyra met and the one she fell in love with, not imagining that he, having grown up with no adversity himself, would not stay that way very long. His childhood was spent in an intact family, in material comfort, wrapped in pleasant manners and attractive surroundings. All those things nurtured his confidence in himself and a habit of seeking attractive women without hesitation. That's also why he ridiculed hearts that were wounded and was inclined to go after new relationships: to indulge in pleasantries with the innocence of an absolutely sincere man, a good friend, who simply follows the impulses of his new desire.

He wanted lots of friends and that meant he learned to hide his real spiritual essence behind small talk. He learned to stay cool and was extremely easy to get along with, even among people with different values. He realized that he contradicted himself sometimes when he defended things that he would normally condemn. While he was under the influence of business partners with whom he worked, who were both good and noble, Steponas never imagined that at some point he would slip quite easily into satisfying his waywardness.

Blinded by his wonderful, attractive appearance, Elvyra didn't imagine this side of him. Unfortunately, it came out and Elvyra was horribly disappointed. Still, she didn't understand the source of her frustration, but she felt it was wrong that Steponas was the way he was, and he would not be a strong contributor to a harmonious family. It wasn't that she wanted a steady ground under her feet for herself alone – by no means. If she were single and saw Steponas seeking the company of other women, she would have gotten out of his way and gone to raise a family working for her parents.

But she had children with Steponas. "And who would give us a divorce, or even any judgement," she said, "Because we have children!" Splitting up the children was abhorrent to her. Even if her husband left all of them in her custody, wouldn't it hurt them to have a father who rejected them?

"How would it be," she wondered about modern ways, "if we had a society where the state guarantees every newborn baby a stable childhood and a secure life. In this view, children would become the children of society. Society would be the provider for their welfare and the goal of its work, and people wouldn't see a big difference between their own children and others. Everyone would worry about all of them equally. Would people in this kind of system marry once and for their whole lives? Would they enter into longer or shorter committed relationships? Probably most people would be taken over by their primitive instincts and only a few commitments would persist, those that are more selective and strong.

"The masses will always surrender to the oldest instinct to multiply or essential ways to avoid becoming extinct. Only rare, exceptional people will look forward with more nuance and with greater effort, to put a greater value on love and to put a greater importance on good works for society, in the service of enabling successful people.

"These individuals will be less likely to do things the usual way, the ordinary way of tending to the species—reproducing intensively. Their goal will be to create an environment in which the younger generation will have a strong position in the struggle for natural existence, safe from degeneration or ruin!"

While thinking out loud, Elvyra saw that she wasn't worried as much about her own welfare, but sad for the children, and that by working through these terrible thoughts, the hardest question to answer was what will happen to their progeny.

Breaking the Mold

What did Steponas do? When he saw that his wife was trying to be nice to him, now that she felt somewhat beaten down and grateful to get part of her husband back, he explained what he needed: *She's insensitive and does everything 'out of duty.' I had a completely different childhood. It's not surprising that from early on I refused to be fenced in and follow rules or accept obligations, and headed off toward freedom...*

It seemed to Steponas that it would help keep Elvyra happy if his only obligation was to avoid flirting in front of her and not irritate her. But when he was out of sight, he felt no duty to restrain himself, since he would be "going against his own nature" which was in conflict with morality.

Literature at that time bolstered this belief of his. It led him to wade even more deeply into the mud of flirtation and oblivion. And the more he went in that direction, the further he moved from Elvyra, until finally even he could see it. At times, he was overcome and undone with the fear that he was digging his own grave and sometimes he felt that he should turn to Elvyra, seek out her sympathy and common ground. Elvyra always comforted him and warmed to him again, and it eased both their hearts.

During those kinds of moments, his flirting seemed like a bad dream to Steponas. He would've been happy if some of the memories turned into mere events he'd dreamed. All the more when he saw how much everyone appreciated Elvyra and didn't doubt that the two were suited for each other. Unfortunately, those moments were brief and came up only when there were questions about marriage or love, which exposed a fundamental difference in his approach to morals.

All of that caused Steponas great consternation, which in turn upset Elvyra. She couldn't stay indifferent when it brutally pulled the strings of her sensitive heart. Every flair of the matter of their mutual pain ended in Elvyra's tears and Steponas' vehement outbursts. He accused her of being "dried-up, cold-natured, unsympathetic to him, subconsciously clinging to obsolete theories." As he tore their good relationship apart again, Steponas sought comfort and diversion elsewhere, from women who wanted to seduce a man like him – admired and well-known for having a beautiful and smart wife.

Some of the women, feeling victorious in their conquest, tried to take the affair to its conclusion, meaning to separate Steponas from his wife and take her place. They sought this goal with no conscience and raw ambition, but, it seemed, they were wrong. Indeed, Steponas fell into their traps, dreaming of a private tryst, but failing to ponder that that step could ruin him and the family of a woman who was married.

He often said that there was no harm and would be no harm if a married man flirted with a married woman. It was different when an opportunist courted a single young woman. Then he could ruin her life and end up in a different direction. According to him, two people who desire each other and are members of different families can freely give in to their feelings and do not, because of that, have to derail the marriage to the cheated spouse, because people can love more than one person in life.

He proclaimed this belief even with respect to Elvyra. However, he was much devoted to her, and respected her, that the thought of separating from her never came to mind. In truth, he was too respectful to cross the ultimate boundary in secret. He didn't want to feel guilty even in his own eyes. He felt terrible about even small indulgences that he allowed himself, squeezing a small hand or some other form of affection, that he would spoil his pleasant mood and couldn't relax socially. Nevertheless, not used to blaming himself, he pitied Elvyra and accused her of failing to approach life with intelligence and not allowing him to desire freely, while she remained his wife and friend. It seemed to him that in cases where he didn't hide anything from her, he could allow himself a moment of indulgence and allow the desire to evolve into forbidden love.

This attitude toward his proposal seemed reasonable. And too, he was weary of the constant internal conflict and the struggle with surging desire, that he couldn't even come close to understanding Elvyra. He could only feel sorry for himself and simply thought about what was good for him. Blinded by selfishness, he snapped at Elvyra ever more often. Here she was led by theories and yet would not accept a life in which he was what he was. As spouses, compared to other couples, they were perfectly suited to one another. If she would only look at life rationally, they would be the happiest of people and the best of friends.

For Elvyra, this view provoked endless anxiety. She couldn't understand what he was talking about; she just felt some kind of impending doom. It was hard to bring herself to do her daily routines. She had to try to appear to be calm. She was wide awake for whole nights, gaunt and exhausted.

Steponas, busy with his own business, didn't even notice. Once, he ran into her in a pasture and said:

"I see that you're content with your life's purpose and happy with it. I'm different. I wasn't built to be monogamous. It's torture for me."

Pain stabbed through Elvyra's heart. It meant that Steponas was blind to her suffering and although she tried hard not to constrain him, he felt distressed, deprived?! What more did he want from her? What?

She decided to ask him directly.

"Tell me, Steponas," she said, "If you feel such pain living with me, and part of you has to deal with me, tell me straight and honestly, what am I not giving you? We can't go on this way. I feel more pain now than you do!"

Out of the blue Steponas begged relief from the weight of depression, and with incorrigible boldness laid out for his wife everything he'd hidden from her for so long. His confession finished:

"In your mind, you look at me now as if I were guilty and you don't see that in spite of everything, I'm better than most men, because others in my place would quietly deceive you all the way, and you'd live under the illusion that you've got the best, most faithful husband. I'm all too genuine and sincere, even though I consider it foolish. You know I could easily walk all over your uncompromising point of view and live in harmony with my nature. It's strange that on your side you want to separate from me over nothing. You well know," he spoke, spelling out every word, "that we two cannot live without the other, and I won't find a better wife anywhere.

"Our divorce would shock the whole world, because everybody, except for you, thinks of us as an exceptionally compatible couple, or something like that. If you take a good look at people, you'd see something like our bond in nearly every family. You can flirt with others if you want, I have nothing against that and don't see anything bad in it. Someday people will understand and won't bother each other over it. But people who divorce, and yet are close, have children, and are able to be friends – I call that a travesty."

Elvyra listened to him wide-eyed. As Steponas talked she stared at him even more. His last words were especially astonishing. She was struck speechless, unable to say a word, and then before long recovered. She winced and frowned with distress… Finally, her expression was watchful, while deep folds lined her neck.

"You may think I'm crazy or depraved. I don't defend myself nor argue that you're wrong. I know that I'd be extremely offended if I came to learn I was serving as a cover for your consorting with others. That situation is loathsome and I can never agree to it."

"Am I wrong in saying," shouted Steponas, "that appearances and facades are more important to you than substance? You're deep into principles, and by clinging to them you want to ruin your life and mine! But trust me," he said ever more heated, "People will soon be free from these damn forms. Maybe even now we're in a transition period."

"If you think," Elvyra cut in, "That that kind of behavior is ethical and moral, then tell me, why aren't you clearly happy with your own success in that department? Why do you hide every time you behave that way, as if you believed that you were behaving in the wrong and causing pain?"

"I hide," Steponas answered, "Because people haven't progressed to being as free as I want to be. They don't understand me and condemn me for no reason."

"Those poor people!" sighed Elvyra with suppressed irony. But that wasn't a stick she wanted to use in the fight. After a second of despair she said, "Steponas, think of me what you want, but I can't live with you anymore. Tomorrow my friends and relatives are going to know. Do whatever you want. You won't hurt me, because, I won't be your wife."

Her message was broken by tears pouring from her eyes as she cried.

"I'll stay under your roof, if that's okay, because I don't want to separate you and the children. But I won't be your wife and the lady of this house any more. From now on I'll just tend to the children. I don't have the energy for anything else... However, I'm not captive; I have the right to be independent any time – at least the same right!" She huddled in anguish and resolve, as she saw worry in Steponas' eyes. She was afraid he would start to argue and try to convince her that she couldn't do what she wanted to.

On hearing such harsh words, Steponas grasped for the first time that Elvyra wasn't his property – something he could freely throw away – but a person with her own will. He looked at Elvyra and was astonished! She'd held her beauty beyond all others. He saw her as he had long ago – unusually attractive and desirable. He started to understand that he'd mistreated her. She wasn't his belonging, but an independent person with her own personal rights.

How badly, very badly, he'd treated her.

He gently hugged his wife and as tenderly as he could, said:

"Okay, Elvyra. Let's do what you want. We'll live as if we were separated. We'll test our own love and the love between us. We'll see if we can each live without the other. There's just one thing I ask: let's define how long for this trial

– for example, two months. And during that time, let's not tell anyone about it and go on living the way we are."

Elvyra agreed right away. It wasn't easy for her to carry out the decision she'd pronounced, with her own family. A pause was also needed because she wanted to get used to the new situation, that way, she'd have enough energy, at the right time, to reveal her sorry lot to their peers.

The conversation between the two of them took place in the garden, sitting on the bench. Having reached an agreement, each had a lighter heart. Elvyra calmly thought about her new situation. From time to time Steponas glanced at her with curiosity. Elvyra stood up first and wanted to leave.

"Wait," Steponas held her back. "Please don't run away from me!"

Not quite understanding what he meant by that entreaty, Elvyra paused for a minute. Encouraged by her wavering, Steponas took her by the hand.

"Give me your sweet hand, my poor dear..." he whispered with feeling, and then stopped, puzzled by Elvyra's withdrawal.

"No, Steponas," She pulled her hand away and spoke with a sad but firm voice. "I'm not going to stop halfway. Remember, we don't belong to each other anymore!... It's time to see what the children are doing."

She hurried back towards the house.

Distress

Left alone, Steponas sat and thought. So, they've quit each other! So, she won't do things half way! It seems just as she said, she's ready to get out of his way. And she'll do it, really do it, with not a bit of protest, no more scolding, blaming fate or their mutual tragedy. Nevertheless, he didn't intend get divorced! Not for the world… If only he wouldn't lose her, not for anything.

When he thought about the children, Steponas realized what a sorry situation they were in, with parents who are fighting. The thought nearly brought him to tears. He was overcome with a sadness he wanted to escape as soon as possible. He wasn't used to this kind of gloom. He went back to the house to work on something.

But the work dropped from his hands. He leaned on the writing table and tried to drown his thoughts. These thoughts went to the woman who had become the reason for his disagreement with Elvyra. After all, he wasn't seeing her as a lifelong friend! He felt an extraordinary passion for her, but at the same time clearly saw her feminine weaknesses. She had the same feelings he did, but she was better at using her mind to control her feelings. She loved him and didn't hide it. She was warm, seeking intimacy without a heavy heart.

Looking back brought back all the times when she did good or bad things without a thought, or acted like they were courting. Sometimes she was pleased with herself that she'd cleverly succeeded in separating an unwelcome person from their circle of friends and thereby won the two of them a time of happiness. She understood life and knew what it gave her – both happiness and comfort. After all, wasn't she trying to create trouble in her home or his? To tell the truth, he never brought it up with her and generally didn't like to say Elvyra's name in front of her. Why? He couldn't explain that to himself, and never thought about it.

His thoughts drifted again to his wife and children. Elvyra had a right to respond as her values commanded. But her views were also unfortunate. She utterly did not understand human nature! From the time she became his wife, there were to be no temptations. She held firm to conventional rules and protected her saintly reputation, that there would never be the slightest stray desire that would be contrary to the prescriptions of the code of aristocracy. He wouldn't force her to, if she didn't want to. If after this conversation, she wanted to divorce him, then they would separate permanently.

He remembered how distressed she was, tearfully pulling her hand away from his and running off into the pasture. She often came to the same pasture to help him… The significance of that memory made him sad, so upset, that he decided that very minute to hurry to Elvyra to promise to break his ties to others, to reconcile and to make sure he wouldn't lose her. He glanced at his watch. It was late – why hadn't they called him to supper?... His desire to see Elvyra was upsetting and he needed to run off to find her.

The servant told him that she'd taken the path to the birch grove. He grabbed a hat and went toward it. In the forest that covered a graceful hill, Elvyra sat on a log in the high grass. When she heard him coming, she jumped up to go.

"It's really late," she said uneasily, "for you to look for me here. I didn't realize it was already evening."

"The time has run away from me too, Elvyra, while I thought about things. I spent a lot of time in my study. It's no wonder you can forget the whole world there. I came to talk to you... Elvyra, I can't be apart from you more than a few hours. I can't. I don't want you to leave me. I don't want to be kept from touching you. I don't want to feel separate from you forever – from you and the children. My Elvyra ... I feel that it would hurt me too much to lose you. I'll do everything to get back your love."

Elvyra cried. He hugged her tight and kissed her.

"Why are you crying?... Tell me... I give you my word, I'm finished with others. Is that enough for you? Do you really believe me?... What else do you want?"

"You're strange, Steponas, imagining things! Are your promises enough for me? Do they give me a guarantee? As for your ideas, your values that are so different from my ethical standards? You aren't going to change them in one fell swoop. Those relationships – those aren't business contracts, and you can't pull away from them the same way. Do you think 'she' won't be hurt? I'm sure she's not just attracted to you – she wants to become your wife, especially because you're a better catch than her current husband."

"Your opinion of her surprises me," interjected Steponas. "One way or another, she's in competition with you. But I know her very well and can venture to say that she has nothing like that in mind. She wants to get out of life what it offers. That's all."

"Please spare me any competition. I refuse all of it, ever," snapped Elvyra as if stung, and stood up. "I give you up to her and all the rest, who can rouse your lust! I haven't the slightest desire to engage in any foolishness like that. What do we have in common? I don't want any more…"

In another minute, she continued:

"Excuse me. I'm too tired to think or talk clearly. Why did you come here? Why were you looking for me? I have a headache… I want to be alone, quiet."

She choked from crying.

"I came," said Steponas calmly, "because I wanted to make up. I still want to, in spite of your crazy talk. That's why, whether it suits you or not, I say again: I'll stop getting involved with that woman for good. If in spite of that you still don't want to get along, remember – if the children suffer, it'll be your fault."

"I told you," said Elvyra, "I'll wait to see how your new promises turn out, with patience, and I'll hold to my word. Right now, I just want to be calm and quiet."

After they had this conversation and parted, neither could sleep for a long time.

The scene replayed in Steponas' mind: what will happen when he tells the other woman that he wants to leave her for good? He was afraid she wouldn't really understand his point of view and would continue to confront him, and reproach him for giving in to his wife's whims. The thought hurt his pride. The fear of a public scandal tormented him.

Elvyra on the other hand didn't see a wonderful future for herself, her husband, or her children, again. The two lovers had thought they would never hurt anyone and they were just two people close to each other. Steponas, pushed to break up his relationship with the other woman, will feel that he's sacrificed himself, and will yearn for the one he left, dream of her. How will they go on after this break in their relationship?

A Turn

Steponas did not rush to quit his lover, postponing it over and over again with the hope that the right time would come up. And because that never seemed to happen, he decided not to wait any longer. He drove to the town where the lady lived. Her husband wasn't home. That's why he came upon an acquaintance in the company of his beloved, a young engineer, who'd finished his studies the year before and worked in the town. The lady friend immediately and cleverly got rid of the young man and, wild with enthusiasm was all over Steponas in the next minute. He gently pulled away and asked her to sit down and listen. Her expression was worried, looming with foreboding.

"You look the sky has fallen. Did somebody find us out?"

"Nobody found us out. I came to tell you that we've got to quit. Our situation can hurt my children and yours."

"My dear," she said sharply, "You should've thought what would happen to the children long before now. Even so, everything can be managed. I only have daughters and they'd stay with me. But you have three sons, whom you'll keep with you, and leave the daughter with your wife. Are we the first people to get divorced? There are statutes and conventions. People who don't find happiness in one marriage find it in another."

Steponas was infuriated by the cruel re-engineering of his domestic life, and by her self-confidence.

"How do you know I'm not happy with Elvyra?" he stung back.

"It speaks for itself: if you'd found love there, would you be looking for it with me? If you didn't intend to leave her, then why are you bothering me and ruining my good name? Oh please, dear. And now you want to break up. You don't have a right to be so dismissive of me."

"Listen," sputtered Steponas, barely suppressing his rage, "You can't blame me for everything. You're no amateur, and we're the same age. You're responsible for your reputation and your own peace of mind. As to whether I have a right to break it off now, tell me first, did either of us have the right to betray our spouses: your husband, my wife?"

The lady friend, finding no good argument, started to sob bitterly and then swoon and scream hysterically as if she wanted to raise the roof. Steponas, composed, leaned over and said, seriously,

"If you don't want to completely lose your dignity, then stop this scandalous fit. You're not going to gain anything by it."

The comment calmed her. She stood up, hissed "You cad!" through gritted teeth, and left the room.

The extreme pathetic rage opened Steponas' eyes. He'd imagined their break-up quite differently! He watched her cry over the lost love and babbling, giving into hopeless wailing with grief. It's as if he'd collided with a furious and vindictive egotist with no respect for herself. Left disgusted and aggrieved from that scene, he slowly lightened up that it was over.

Tired from lack of sleep and drained from the ugly experience, even darker thoughts pierced his mind. He stole back home full of worry which only worsened when he didn't find Elvyra in the bedroom even though it was already midnight. He didn't ask the servants and decided to find her himself.

While her husband went out, Elvyra felt short of breath indoors and walked out to the pasture and sat on the bench under the oak tree in spite of the late hour. She was torn to shreds with awful feelings. The image of Steponas at his lady friend's house – how he looked at her, oblivious, come for whatever, submitting to her luring caresses, thereby destroying Elvyra's home and happiness, and her children's.

"How much more damage can one shameful act deliver!" she thought. "Pain goes out from that heart in all directions, touching everything hot or cold. Why, for example, hurt the little ones? They might reject their father. How awful…" She felt sorry for Steponas. Sorry he was blind and failed to open his eyes. Suddenly she heard footsteps. Steponas appeared in front of her.

"Why aren't you in bed? Why are you sitting here in the dark?" he asked, quietly surprised, speaking with distant and heavy voice like a depressed person. He dropped next to her on the bench. Elvyra didn't answer. Her awful feeling wasn't gone. Even though it was dark, she could see him sitting beside her, close to her, but with such a cold heart! She waited for him to speak, like a criminal waiting for a sentence.

"What are you thinking?" Steponas asked with sadness. "I thought you honestly trusted me and would be happy I came back. Everything's ended with the other one! You were right – she expected to get married. Her reaction pulled the veil from my eyes. I'm completely cured…"

Elvyra's wounded heart couldn't cheer up. She continued to sit still, not even reaching out to her husband. After Steponas' words her spirit was lighter, but her weary mind and nerves had a right to relax in relief. A sweet dizziness washed over her. She swayed in a faint. Worried about her energy, Steponas gently put his arm around his wife. Elvyra leaned her head on his chest, and Steponas felt that although she was still upset and hurt, he still had her, he hadn't lost her.

Overcome with exhaustion and the need to sleep, Elvyra led her husband home.

After that their relationship got more measured, better, warmer, in spite of occasional angry words due to their different views of morality. As before everyone considered them a strong couple. They appreciated Elvyra more and more, and Steponas took pride in his wife. After that Elvyra concluded that married life – the way society wanted it – degenerates when the impulse to procreate gets out of hand. She tried to modify the way they lived and was soon pleased to see her thinking bear fruit.

Everyday experiences go by like reflexes and we are not conscious of them. But because the greatest happiness comes to us only consciously, we have to watch for negativity everywhere it could flourish.

There's no happiness without struggle! Because happiness – it's a win, a moment of victory. When Steponas passionately desired his wife, he was the most sensitive. There was only one thing missing in his marriage: the wish he'd expressed before, to taste forbidden fruit, to flirt.

A Warm Guest

Elvyra thought things over when she sat in front of the mirror in her nightgown. She thought about the present. It wasn't very long ago that Mykolas had come to visit and already she felt a warm respect for him. She felt that he delighted in everything he saw in her. Of course, it was enormously pleasing. *There's nothing wrong with a little admiration,* she thought. *Also, it's a good thing, because appreciation makes us a better person. I'd be thrilled if Steponas truly respected an honest and moral woman, because a good, smart and decent woman can't be influenced to be bad, to spoil someone else's nest and or even just steal a friend. Like Anupras Zodeika, who's admired me a lot, for a long time. His family hasn't suffered for it, and even gotten good things from it. Didn't I show Zodeika how to cherish his wife, whom he really treasures?*

Zodeika admired Elvyra like people admire a piece of art. Just the thought of looking at her as a woman seemed inappropriate, heretical. Lady Zodeika who with her husband liked Elvyra and mixed socially never once told her that it was good to know that Elvyra was no threat to her. On the contrary, her husband's devotion to Elvyra was insurance against his moral transgressions. Elvyra was an unusually virtuous woman who saw it her duty to help people improve their lives and thought that those who were stronger had an obligation to help those weaker.

Steponas came on his wife in this frame of mind, to say good-night.

"My philosopher hasn't gone to bed yet?" he asked her, warmly and sweetly. He stroked her hair and thoughtfully looked her in the eyes. Pleased to hear Mykolas' praise for her, he wanted to understand, to guess, what charmed his friend so much. He looked her over like a familiar but forgotten toy that suddenly seemed precious and significant.

"My wife seems to have turned Mykolas' head. I'm sure it's not the philosophy but those eyes," he said, kissing her eyes. Steponas completely agreed with Mykolas – his wife was worth admiring. And he was in no way jealous. He trusted Elvyra too much to give in to jealousy. Quite the opposite, he was happy that a sophisticated man from Warsaw admired his wife and for that win he was effusive with love, as you might reward a child for a good job with homework.

The improved rapport with Elvyra brought about a greater sense of contentment in her and a happiness that showed in her appearance. It made her more beautiful. The time she was free from everyday chores she spent with Mykolas, as their guest. And then Steponas, with whom Mykolas didn't succeed in discussing the farm or horses, left the job of entertaining him to Elvyra. Mykolas forthwith took every opportunity to have a talk with Elvyra. He knew when she went for a walk, when she toured the farm. Whenever he could, he would try to accompany her somewhere or look after her some way.

One very warm day after dinner, they sat in the living room.

"Imagine, Sir," she said, speaking of her ideas about the world, "if there were no living creatures in our world, just various inorganic forms and just the beginnings of movement everywhere: chaotically flowing, colliding, crashing into each other, smashing as they succumb to the law of gravity. As one of these cells strikes another, it doesn't try in the least to avoid the adverse collision. That's a 'deadly embrace.' And when a living entity meets its extinction against an alien organism or an inorganic object, it subconsciously tries to avoid it and tries to find a way to meet in a way that's productive. That's a 'kiss of life,' or sensation. Our whole world is composed of the variety resulting from this encounter. When we say: red, odorous, brilliant, dull, sonorous, cold, hot, beautiful, awful – they're all identifiers differentiated by their encounter with stages in the external world."

"By your theory, vegetation has to be assigned to the inorganic world, because it can neither avoid contact with other objects, nor seek it."

"How so? Don't plants try to move, when they sprout and bend toward the sun, when they send roots under rocks, looking for better soil!"

"Sure, that's true. But we often cut grass, and it can't avoid hostile contact with the scythe."

"You're wishing for forbidden things. After all, even humans can't anticipate all dangers. In nature, the most important impulse is to persist and to stay alive. It's enough to observe the remarkable fact that plants try to obtain the most advantageous environment in life, that is, 'the kiss of life,' or sensation. If we take that criterion to be the instinct for survival, it would be understandable as some kind of expression of life. Any living creature, anywhere and always, given life, chooses an environment in which it can live. That is to say superficially it seeks the most suitable environment. Creatures sprang spontaneously or by adaptation from one-celled organisms, that we call plants, animals and finally humans. Every one of them finds its evolutionary path and tries to reach its ultimate goal."

"In other words, everything that is alive wants to stay alive, but not everything has the same ability to adapt on its evolutionary path. Is that what you wanted to say?"

"You don't have to explain a lot to someone smart," she answered with an amiable smile. "I should learn from your insights. But I can't resist saying that our will – will, that people are used to calling 'free,' is nothing but the kiss of life, which is so free that in most cases it's unconscious, simply the momentum of energy striving for the goal."

Out in Nature

After spending a month at Egliai, Mykolas felt better than he had anywhere else. Until then he never imagined how much his friendship with Elvyra could mean to him. He lived for every day that he could listen to her, feel close to her, trying to see her as often as possible. Often, he pursued her like a young man, and that got the attention of Steponas, and after a while it annoyed him. Mykolas brought her flowers in the morning and was as delighted as a child when, once in a while, she took a blossom and put it in her hair. Sometimes they spent time sharing memories of childhood, or told each other of various adventures from school days: Elvyra about her family, about when and how she got to know Steponas, whereas Mykolas told about his beloved sister, who died of consumption a few years earlier. Once he asked:

"Do you know that it's only here in Egliai that I've come to know what real love is?"

Hearing such a fairly blunt and astonishing statement, Elvyra blushed and was truly concerned. Wanting to hide her disloyal blush, she tried to give Mykolas the benefit of the doubt.

"It seems to me that you may love, but you might be wrong about what you imagine to be the nature of true love."

But Mykolas didn't admit he was wrong. He saw her blushing cheeks and wanted to be sure that if Elvyra didn't admit she loved him, at least she could know the truth

81

looking into his eyes. That's why he shamelessly gazed into her eyes, openly, and in doing it aroused in her heart an even greater alarm.

Nevertheless, from that moment Mykolas felt that Elvyra's behavior changed. She toned down with him and wasn't as free. He became more subdued. He racked his brains how to let Elvyra know that his feelings were not out of line and that he could never disrespect a woman like her. He wanted to tell her, but he couldn't decide when to bring up the topic – he lost his nerve at the last minute.

Whereas Elvyra was quite uneasy for a while. She couldn't understand why she played such a big part in Mykolas' feelings, at all. She enjoyed seeing his elegant presence often beside her, sensing how thoughtful he was toward her, giving her his total attention. When he looked at her she felt quite beautiful and really delighted to serve him or accommodate his preferences. He made her very happy to feel understood and have him listen to her with interest!

She'd always been critical of herself, and now she recognized that Mykolas made a strong impression to her. Maybe she reacted like that because Steponas hadn't paid attention to her for such a long time? Surely, she knew about life and was perfectly suited to him – why would such a forbidden feeling awake in her?! It seems that anyone can stray this way, but not everyone knows how to redeem the situation. For sure, Steponas was still dear and beloved, and his love was as important as ever to her!

Elvyra was troubled by these kinds of questions. Her fear grew as she admitted to herself that once in a while she wasn't as sad about things that had tormented her recently. She didn't complain that Steponas didn't seem as happy with her as she would have liked. Did the change happen because he was different towards her now? He was ever more attentive, becoming kinder and more sensitive. Certainly, Mykolas had something to do with it! Steponas, sensing competition, had to make an effort, and this came back to him in good ways, improving their relationship with each other.

Elvyra was one of those people who aren't afraid to look reality in the eye. She could calmly analyze her own darkest and innermost feelings and measure them against the experience of Steponas or other acquaintances. Because the way people act is based on great and small experiences in life, and they have stronger and weaker ways to express themselves, there have to be allowances made for the angry and the sinful. She firmly believed that the harder someone tried to be good and serve society, the happier they would be, because fighting and defeat – are based in the principles of nature and the mysteries of happiness.

A little after dinner the children asked their mother to go boating with them at Venta River. It was a hot day, the whole cloud cover hanging ethereally like a spider web, with sunlight coming down as if blocked, through frosted glass – just pale light. Elvyra agreed and with Vytautas, and Mykolas hanging back not one step, went to the river. Because she liked to navigate she sat down next at the tiller, and Mykolas sat in front of her with the youngest children beside him. Vytautas sat on the last bench and took the oars. After him Jasius sat in the end of another boat.

The water was undulating, rolling away gracefully in front of them, here and there landing neatly against the sandy shores of the Venta River. Sometimes the river narrowed and flowed as if through a lane of hazel, oak and ash trees, until it again passed into a wider channel or strained through cattails. In places the shore was flat and opened up on

83

amazing vigorous grasses surrounding a deep lagoon. These meadows were the wide summer channels of the Venta, the shore being further out at that time.

Mykolas saw this beautiful setting for the first time, because he hadn't gone as far as the "desert island" before. He was mesmerized. Elvyra was energized by the natural beauty as well.

"The shores of the Venta take your breath away," he said. "Do you know why this view is full of life like this, a scene that makes people feel younger?"

"Because we're here," said Elvyra, simply.

"Oh, but all I see is you..." whispered Mykolas in such a way that Vytautas wouldn't hear and gazed at her figure with fiery eyes.

Although the sun was behind clouds it was stifling and humid – hard to catch your breath up against the overhang of steep shorelines. Elvyra felt lethargic from the air and her critical mind which was normally sharp got a little drowsy. Inattentive, her lips barely open to breathe, she listened to Mykolas' whisper and didn't quite get what he was saying. She loved his ardent look. The heat and the rhythm of the oars were putting her to sleep. It seemed she was dreaming with her eyes open. All her senses were subdued, but one – attraction to Mykolas.

Mykolas sat in front of her, then he leaned forward a little, bracing his right hand on the side of the boat, and lowered a hand in front of him as if wanted to give her something. The sight of his hand caught Elvyra off guard. It appeared to her as if he were holding an open palm to receive hers; as if he was going to spring onto his knees toward her and cover her hand with kisses. A shiver went through her, her hand hesitantly stretched out to Mykolas. But right away she caught herself. Her awareness chided her, like a boss just wakened and rousing a loafing worker. She hid her minute of absence, straightened the pleats on her dress, and stared into the distance.

Mykolas didn't notice Elvyra's internal conflict. It seemed to him that such an extraordinary woman wouldn't have common feelings. He wasn't embarrassed when she pulled her hand away very quickly. He didn't understand the abrupt change in her expression or the uneasiness that appeared in her eyes when she answered.

"It's time to go back," Elvyra said with a firm tone. "Jasius, our lessons will be late today," she said to her son. Then, wanting to get past the recovery from a fateful moment, offered to Mykolas: "Maybe you'd like to take over from Vytautas, who's completely worn himself out doing all the rowing. We're going downstream now; it won't be too hard."

The men changed places. Vytautas situated himself in front of Elvyra. She liked to discuss with him the progress Jasius was making in his studies, his talents and various everyday things. When they got home she went to pay full attention to Jasius' lessons. That day, Mykolas only saw her before tea, because she was usually wrapped up in the work of running the household. After tea, she told him that she had to take care of a few things that'd been put off and she disappeared.

Elvyra had neglected some of her chores over the prior months and she wasn't happy with herself. Now with doubled energy she tried to catch up. After she'd worked several hours late into the evening and finished, she couldn't fall asleep for a long time. The image of what had happened in the boat stuck in her mind and she tried to figure it out. In the dark, when the outside world doesn't impinge, it is easier to think about herself and figure out her feelings. Elvyra often paced around the dark living room on cold winter nights, to think about things before she went to sleep.

Am I not in a struggle for both my survival and for the routines that are sustaining my species? she said to herself, vividly recalling how her mind went to sleep and totally went on automatic pilot. *Really, my conscious mind clearly stopped functioning, it seems, because of the heat and stuffiness. I mean, the heat weakened my willpower, which is really my conscious, general awareness. Many things probably happen when we're in nature that make our sophisticated brains and nerve cells go wrong. We need research to look into this phenomenon. It would really help our understanding of real life to know more about risks like this!*

Mykolas has become something that's getting in the way of my thinking. He's wakened my baser instincts, with his constant focus on his own feelings and looking for ways to get close to me all the time. Sure, she thought, *the entire mass of my physical cells that haven't each developed independently and haven't developed complex structures such that they could serve the survival of my organism with intelligence and utility – they're old, primordially existing to save the species on the level of the lowest organism – mostly the path of fertility.*

That's the only way to account for and explain, completely and without a doubt, the internal division, the feeling of constant internal conflict. For if the will seeks a desire to live or to express the instinct for preservation, part of the cells in my body have to split off. Couldn't it be true that the cells that are better at change – they're better aligned – win over those whose adaptation is flawed? After all, intelligent classes lead the ignorant, who if left to themselves would go off in a different direction more suited to their

86

limited abilities. The resilience of humanity depends on self-control, and insight into a situation can ensure success.

She sighed and felt sorry for Steponas.

That means when someone is in conflict, he needs to draw strength from his own predilections or from religion. But if he doesn't have resistance, then he'll succeed only if he was introduced to a sense of right and wrong as a child and self-control is a habit and has become second nature. It's best to raise children from the very beginning to respect people, and foster what we generally call 'a strong will,' to introduce him to everything that he'll need in adversity!

Elvyra thought about the children and their personalities. The youngest Vytukas always failed to finish things he'd started – if any problem came up, his motivation to accomplish what he'd planned disappeared. Where did that come from? How do you cultivate the ability to carry through and handle yourself? How to inspire a strong spirit, in a way that what we call will power is developed, and a child knows how to control his physical impulses? Primarily you have to set goals that are achievable and to try, if necessary, to help him reach them. When habits are formed, you get results. After that you have to teach them further, to reinforce the good of it, reminding them often, until they start to go after the good of it, make it close to them and easy and clear. Instill in them a pressure to be strong!

The Guest Has a Plan

The next day Elvyra got up pale, with deep bags under her eyes. Before she went to the veranda, where breakfast was being served, as usual she met the gaze of the elegant Mykolas, who always greeted her by bowing and kissing her hand. She was bothered that he was oblivious that such a trivial but sensual gesture could lead to something. Instead she warmly greeted him, coolly held out her hand, and immediately started a conversation with her mother, asking her about Maryte's health, as she was not well. Paying no attention to Mykolas, as if he wasn't even there, she ordered a meal of broth and such for her.

After tea, Mykolas, knowing that Elvyra normally walked around the farm at that time, brought her an umbrella and gloves, ready to go with her. But Elvyra thanked him and advised him that she wasn't going out today because she had to get ready for a dance to be held in two days. This excuse was completely reasonable to Mykolas and he wouldn't keep her.

He went to get his own coat, a scarf and gloves. As he was putting them on, he made a mental note to ask her to promise him a Mazurka, and if that went well, a cotillion dance. *But will she agree?* he thought. *Will it make tongues wag?* And what made her strongly attractive to him? After all, he shouldn't expect anything, beyond a warm friendship. But still – he couldn't imagine life without the pleasure of seeing her. He remembered that his vacation was ending and he will have to leave, and that made him depressed. *Isn't it conceivable that sometime in his life he could find work here, near Elvyra? And humanity wouldn't suffer much for it,* he thought. *Without a doubt, he would become an energetic worker if only her sun shone on him.* At that very minute a surprising thing came to his aid.

A Mr. Zodeika was invited to evening supper, and he said with great enthusiasm that if he had the capital, he would locate a peat mine here, near Smiltishkes. Indeed, there was a lot of peat in the area. There was no doubt about the profit for a company – the forests were declining in size, and peat was continually in greater demand as fuel.

Zodeika's idea stunned Mykolas. Because, he had capital and he could invest in something like that. In a second he had a plan: he'll settle here in this area, not far from Egliai, and when the factory is built, he'll certainly be able to visit Egliai. Surely Steponas wouldn't deny a guest.

He talked to Anupras about the details of business like that, and the two of them got excited planning to form a company. Steponas wasn't home at that time, but he intended to draw him into the idea, all the better for maximum peatlands – on his land. When his host and landholder returned, the two investors immediately explained matters to him and negotiated, then waited for his agreement. But he said only, that if there were a loss, he would not cover it.

Elvyra listened in but she didn't meddle in business matters. Whenever Steponas made critical comments about a serious issue, she was only happy inside because she was afraid that Mykolas would overstay his visit with them. She hoped that it would turn out his idea wasn't feasible.

"I'll be thrilled if I'm able to settle down in this region, not far from you," Mykolas said, as he sat down beside her and Mrs. Songailiene. "I would love to hear what the two of you think of my plan?"

Elvyra pretended to be busy pouring tea and didn't answer. Mrs. Songailiene saved her:

"It's a risky business. A noble effort, but risky. I wouldn't advise you to invest your funds in such an unproven, experimental business. Anupras has always been and always will be an optimist and a romantic. It's a blessing he doesn't have money, because he'd lose it. Finally," she said, "you, Sir, aren't a technical person. You have no expertise in business or marketing. You'll have to start up using straight cash. It's a dubious venture, whether the business will pay off. Unless you find a good market for pressed peat."

Mykolas was cool as he politely listened. It was more important for him to know Elvyra's opinion, but he saw that she was silent. He asked again,

"And you?"

"I agree with my mother," Elvyra answered coolly. "You might do better and be more productive getting work in Warsaw, in a literary salon. You'd be independent, and you could freely influence public opinion."

He was hurt by her cold words. *You mean, I'm worthless?* he thought.

"At some point, you said that a person could be productive anywhere and it's important to do something," she said, explaining with irritation, her uneasiness like a shadow across her neck. Elvyra had sympathy for him.

"Still, my words," she said with warmth, "shouldn't influence your decision, and you should do what you think is best."

Her sweet tone calmed Mykolas.

The thought of permanently living not far from Egliai wouldn't go away. *Elvyra can't object to that,* he thought. *Although she's eager to eat the bread of literature, it's only because this extraordinary heart pines for a productive society, thinks least about herself. She's the embodiment of altruism!* He can only be good and useful by helping her. When she understands that, she won't try to send him off to Warsaw, rejected.

Thinking along these lines he wrote a few letters to acquaintances in Warsaw, asking their advice and for materials on dealing with peat.

The day of the party arrived. Steponas' niece Julija Rimsaite arrived having taken the early train from Panevezys District, where she spent the summer with her parents. Miss Julija studied philosophy and history at Zurich University. She was captivating from birth: the way she moved, her big dark eyes, smooth pale complexion, curly blond hair and pretty bright red lips. Unpretentious, approachable, she attracted everyone's admiration and fascination. Her fellow students were in love with her up to their ears, but she, immersed in her studies, knew how to keep a dignified distance, to make sure that none of her secret admirers dared bother her with their declarations of love. Miss Julija was happy to have the eyes of many refined admirers on her above all others. She took for granted that she could win their love with no effort and that her fans were fine with it.

"People are good, and I'm good with them," she said more than once. She liked some men more than others, others less or not at all, but she wasn't in a hurry to choose. Not one was able to rouse passion in her heart.

While having tea in the morning, Elvyra introduced Julija to Mykolas. It was obvious that it put him in the best mood. She didn't get the feeling that he compared the two of them. She was aware that maybe the beauty of her youth was outdone, but sensed right away that she, Elvyra, would not in the least leave his heart.

Mykolas still found no opportunity to act on his intention to commit Elvyra to dance a Mazurka. He feared that if he didn't act on it at home, then others would beat him to it at the party, when Elvyra arrived in the hall. A moment came when she went out into the garden alone. He sidled up to her.

"I have a big favor to ask," he said simply.

"What is it? I'm listening."

"May I dance a Mazurka with you?"

Elvyra put her hand to her neck. A slight smile played on her lips.

"What's your hurry? I'm not even sure if I'm going to be dancing yet," she said, smelling a few roses she'd just picked. "I'm going to want to watch out for Julija and I'll want to make sure she has partners. These days, it seems there aren't enough."

"Miss Julija can't be short on partners... And you have no right to put me off and decline a dance. I won't know anyone there. I'll be alone among strangers. I'm really shy. I'll have no fun at the party without you!"

"I know, Mykolas," she answered, blushing a little. "that sometimes you can't help but make a joke. Please watch out," she added, "I know how to be angry."

Mykolas rushed to apologize and ask her again. Finally, Elvyra promised him a Mazurka, but only on the condition that there were many partners and Julija was not lacking for one.

Party

The dance was all set. It was held in Uzventis, at the home of Butkevicius who had no children. The couple was older, sociable and nice. He was famous for outstanding vodka infusions. She, for her admirable domestic management, tact, and refinement. The Uzventis estate was grand, perfectly suited for entertaining. There were two huge living rooms, a wonderful dining room, and a glassed-in veranda.

When Steponas and his wife, Julija, Mykolas and Vytautas entered the banquet room, they almost swooned, mesmerized by the splendor of the home: tasteful, the furniture arranged in harmonious clusters, accented by the greenery of palms and flowers. The colors of the guests' clothing were amazing against the bountiful greenery. The brightly-lit hall looked like a marvelous crown.

Soon an orchestra began to play over the canopy of exotic plants, ringing out a waltz. Worried about his Mazurka, Mykolas found Zodeika and Vytautas and deftly mentioned, as though on behalf of Steponas wife, that they shouldn't forget to offer a dance to Julija because she didn't know anyone here. He didn't have to remind the men a second time: they both jumped up and in the next minutes Julija's dance book was full. Mykolas himself subscribed to the first quadrille, and the other dances were assigned to Zodeika, Vytautas, and other bachelors who were there.

Julija was glowing with delight and never imagined the real reason for her success. She figured it was due to her popularity and beauty. Her dress was made from a pink gauze, with a darker rose in her hair and along her neckline, and her lithe figure graced the waltz – it seemed she was floating above the ground.

Mykolas bowed before Elvyra inviting her to dance. It was the first time it was respectable to be close to her like this. He put his arms around her and felt her hands on his shoulders. Blood rushed to his head. He had to use everything he had to control himself and tame the hot desire that the waltz never end. After he spun her around longer than he should have, he finally seated her in a cozy corner hidden by greenery and stood in front of her fanning himself with his hat. Elvyra spoke first:

"Although it's not nice to give yourself credit, I can't help noticing that Julija is surprisingly and truly the queen of the ball."

"Yes, Miss Julija is indeed very pretty. The dress is quite flattering," said Mykolas. "But to me the queen of the ball is not Miss Julija. The title doesn't belong to a young woman. At best, could we call Miss Julija a princess!..."

Just then someone invited Elvyra to dance. She was very happy to escape such an awkward conversation. She resented Mykolas for being too familiar. On the one hand, knowing someone like Mykolas was flattering to her ego. On the other hand, it was upsetting that he was brash and didn't hide his feelings. *What does he want from me?* she asked herself, worried and trying to remember if she ever gave him encouragement to be overly bold.

Sitting down again, near a patiently waiting Mykolas, she tried to push him away by asking: "Why aren't you dancing? There are more ladies than partners. It's a shame they're scarce!" Hearing that, Mykolas quietly stood up and bowed to her. Elvyra explained to him that she was tired and he should ask someone else.

After the contra-dance, the refrain of a Mazurka played out. Mykolas moved beside Elvyra and sat down next to her. He was quite determined to persuade her that the plans for a peat business were actually going to be successful, and his business in the nearby area would be amazingly productive and useful and would not be a problem for anyone. Now he hoped to convince her only because Anupras, out of respect for Elvyra, was trying to get him to move away and was describing everything again in the darkest colors, just to keep Mykolas from moving to the area.

"Look, you once explained to me," he said, "that in making decisions, we should always consider what will be the benefit to society, right?"

"Yes, I've always said that. So?" said Elvyra, interested after his prologue.

"If we make sure that under certain conditions our work can be most beneficial, barring going up in flames or something else, then don't we have to create those favorable conditions?

Elvyra suspected a trap. She wasn't prepared to answer that kind of question. She thought for a minute, then said:

"All right, if you're sure that you're not wrong in assessing the risks. But often our personal and selfish interests get in the way of our visual horizon. It's not hard to make a mistake if that's the case. Rather than get benefits, you get losses."

"What kind of losses could there be if I, for example, feel that it'd be easier for me to work with people like Steponas, and like you, and I manage that personal motive? I think nothing bad is going to come of it and in this situation, I'm in a good position."

There was a note of impatience in his voice. Elvyra had guessed his real motive. She wanted to stop talking about this uncomfortable subject. She interrupted:

"Mykolas, time will tell what you need to do in the future. Right now, there's no good reason to trouble yourself with this idea rather than having fun and helping other people have fun. You like to dance, don't you? The Mazurka is ending but a Chaconne is playing. Why don't you try this dance with Julija? She's known to be outstanding in the solo parts."

"Maybe you'll not refuse to dance the Chaconne with me?"

"Oh, no, no! I just like to watch it. I don't go for solo dances. They're not right for someone my age, anyway."

"Your age?... Now I really don't want to do that dance," said Mykolas and sat down again.

"Oh, you're being difficult. Stop. You're making excuses just to avoid going anywhere. Don't waste time. Please…" she pressured him.

"If you say so, I'm going," Mykolas answered and was soon standing with Julija, waiting for the next refrain.

He was tall, well-built and suave. He danced with dignity and grace, drawing even more attention to Julija's playful movements, which were fluid and effortless. Other couples dancing quickly moved aside to avoid being compared to them. And all eyes in the salon were drawn to Julija and Mykolas.

Mykolas had learned the dance by chance: during a visit to Vilnius his friends took him to a dance class. It wasn't a dance fashionable in the salons in Warsaw.

Julija, feeling all eyes on her, overcame her shyness and put her whole heart into the flow of the music. Her willowy, graceful body looked ethereal. Her partner held his own in style and grand masculine moves. Together they created something amazing and special.

Watching them, Elvyra thought they would be a great couple for life: "If he doesn't get involved with some foolish things not knowing what he wants, will he be able to resist Julija's charms? It seems to me that she would easily respond to his affection."

Elvyra sighed. Although she sincerely wished happiness for Julija, she couldn't deny that she too was nice, and despite Julija's youth and beauty, his attention was on her. *And why do I like that?* she asked herself. Elvyra's pensiveness drew Julija over. Happy, glowing, she ran over to share that she was having an amazing time.

"You know, Auntie, it's fabulous to dance with such a good partner like Mr. Mykolas. You were very nice to invite me to the ball. I've never had such fun!"

The party had special meaning for Julija. Like any young person, she was quick to take every opportunity to venture out and try something new. Moving around she constantly found new surroundings and learned something in them useful to her, making her stronger. That was why children and young people like all kinds of new and different things, every kind of activity – they're instinctively drawn. Julija was happy and congenial at the party, because her success in the eyes of everyone was now guaranteed: her vague dreams about love had come true, a subconscious wish to continue the species. The proximity of success inspires us, whereas the fear of defeat is debilitating and crushing.

Everyone's fascination for Julija, who was unanimously named the queen of the ball, made Mykolas pay more attention to her. The atmosphere of the party was intoxicating to him, meanwhile he'd chatted with Elvyra and had the flames of his flirtation smothered. Gradually he started to act as if he wanted to engage Julija's affection. Mykolas had everything a man needed to appeal to women. His demeanor was highly refined simplicity. And then, the fact that he was a writer and known as a man of literature gave him even more appeal in the eyes of any brides-to-be.

Julija liked him from their first meeting. Now she was beyond thrilled to be seen at the ball with him at her side. Mykolas with his experienced eye got the message immediately and wanted very much to use it for his purposes.

"What if I try to make Elvyra jealous? Maybe then she'll try to get closer to me instead of pushing me away?" He mulled over these disagreeable thoughts and decided to be very sweet to Julija especially in front of Elvyra.

Julija stayed in Egliai for some time after the party because she was having such a good time. Mykolas was very nice to her the whole time. Just one thing made her mad: he was too decent with her—he could be her cousin or her uncle. She didn't know how to explain it to herself but she sensed that he didn't seem concerned about what she thought of him. He seemed indifferent that something would put her off, in other words, what she felt for him, he didn't feel for her. At times, he seemed to actually forget that she was beside him. He would drift off into thought or become oddly distracted. And he was completely different when he talked to her aunt or talked about her! Then he was always considerate and attentive.

"He's afraid of offending her," thought Julija, "And he thinks I'm a child, even though I'm twenty years old." A gloom settled in her heart.

Seeing all that, Elvyra was pleased from the very beginning when she thought Mykolas was succumbing to Julija's charms. But before long she realized she was wrong and decided to have a frank talk with him soon and draw attention to his poor behavior. This awareness made her feel sorry for Julija, because she noticed her mood and was afraid that she harbored false hopes. It was hard to initiate this talk and she put it off every day. Sometimes while the three of them sat in the same place – she, Julija and Mykolas, the conversation turned to art and beauty. Julija held two wonderful roses in her hand. Many grew in Egliai. Those particular roses had just been presented to her and Elvyra by Mykolas.

"It makes sense that a rose is called the queen of flowers," said Julija. "Such a wonderful blossom and amazing smell. You can feel really happy if you smell a rose and look at it."

"Interesting," said Mykolas, looking at Elvyra. "Wouldn't you in this case explain the feeling of happiness as a manifestation of success in the struggle to survive?"

"Didn't we already talk about that? Strange! I usually say things like that early on. I'll say it in the simplest terms: the energy in our bodies is enhanced through things like color, smell, sound and various sensations. A dynamometer will clearly show how much and which colors increase the strength of our muscles. For example, it's known that red is number one in this regard. We always like a surge of energy because it's an advantage in any fight. In other words, when color, smell or taste stimulate our senses, we feel stronger, and that feeling delights us, creating the sensation of happiness. The same way, military music helps us beat fatigue, because the sounds are invigorating and they awaken energy in the muscles."

"Auntie, are you saying that the color and smell of the rose can make a person happy?" asked Julija.

"It could, its freshness can bring back some kind of memory, or, God knows, the mystery of what we generally call beauty. The principle is the same. The stimulus puts us in a state that gives us an experience as if we were waiting for some good news or we're able to help somebody and feel useful. And because we can inherit something abhorrent, or a predilection for something, it's not surprising that we have thousands of these inherited traits. They're quite intertwined with each other, that we can't separate out why one effect gives our muscles energy and others weaken them."

"I think, when you advance your theory, you're certain of all aspects and won't let it be misconstrued, but I'd like to know, how you explain ideal love – love that has no other objective."

"That love doesn't exist," Elvyra snapped back brusquely. "If somebody even imagines that it does, they're naïve. They're not good at appreciating other people or experiencing them."

"Aren't you trying to say that we could admire someone simply because they're good or beautiful? In those cases, there's not a hint of unsavory intention in our minds! Clearly we'd think it was sacrilegious."

Mykolas was talking about himself and his relationship with Elvyra when he made that statement. He really believed what he said and believed that he wasn't looking for any payback and that his feelings were pure. At that moment, he was forgetting his venture that was linked to Elvyra, which was not all that innocent. He forgot how he shook, aroused when she first put her hand on his shoulder to dance with him. He also forgot his passionate hope that she would trust his "pure" feelings, lose her unease about him and reward him for his friendship with gratitude.

Julija didn't understand these insinuations about Elvyra and couldn't see at all why... why was he affectionate in a strange way? Why didn't he want to adore her and seek intimacy with this new lady?... Immensely interested, she sat up and waited to hear what Elvyra was going to say.

"First of all, I have to explain," said Elvyra, "the definitions of 'true love' and 'false love.' In my mind, fertility is the strangest thing in nature, an expression of perpetuity, because that's the way nature strives to propagate a species or have it live on in time. In our political system, which is based on private property, every person has to raise his own children, because the state offers no help.

"Monogamy is the most successful institution in society for socialization. Everyone feels that it's right, instinctively. Religion or the state, which themselves developed out of the instinct for self-preservation, defend monogamy and compel people to observe monogamy threatening various punishments when they don't understand the common social imperative.

"Although some people claim that real fidelity in marriage doesn't exist anymore, nevertheless, up until now society has depended on monogamy. Even unfaithful spouses raise children together. There's no country where children out of wedlock are valued over those in a marriage. Finally, what I call false love is a love that undermines our society and breaks the structure of monogamy in our times."

Mykolas still didn't grasp the crux of her views from what she said and immediately wanted to know where those points were leading.

"Oh sure," Elvyra said as if remembering something, "I don't deny that we can admire goodness or beauty in a person. It isn't love, though, if you don't seek them out to satisfy your desire or even just wish to see them very often. An attraction is just the beginning of greater desire that grows stronger every day and always heads in the same direction – toward one goal. All too often, we see people who're looking for a chance get close to someone they desire but they fool themselves and others because they tell themselves that it's enough to just see the person who incites their passion. Remember Gustav in the poem 'All Souls':

> That's why I wasn't bold enough to sit down
> And didn't ask you to come to love me.
> Please, look at me a little,
> And please stay with me a little,
> Whether as a relative or brother or sister, –
> I wish for more but that's enough.
> Then I can say: I saw her
> And I'll see her the day after and the day after;
> I want to be with her forever, as before,
> When I first said "Hello" at the table –

I would be happy!⁶

"Gustav clung to hope and cursed a world that wouldn't let him have a glimpse of love... In my opinion, people have to help each other, to help them resist the temptations of love where those temptations destroy peace of mind for someone else, and spoil another person's path to love. We have to be careful not to destroy a commitment to a spouse, because that blights society and hurts all humankind. Where the idea of private property is a final stage in the evolution of civilization, the same way monogamy is another absolutely essential element without which we would regress to barbaric times, lose our organic vigor and ultimately, we would disappear from the face of the earth."

Mykolas couldn't and wouldn't be convinced. If he accepted that Elvyra was right, it meant he would lose her and have to stop even seeing her. He resisted this pressure and tried to seize the gravity of the moment with his usual weapon – biting irony.

"I can't agree with you. According to you, society sets such great store by feminine virtue that the minute a woman marries she has to retreat behind four walls and distance herself from others, to avoid any uninvited infatuation. Does that mean everyone around her has to run away from her as if from a leper? That kind of 'flight' has to happen a lot."

Mykolas' ironic tone hurt Elvyra. He saw that and tried to calm her down.

"It seems to me that here you contradict yourself. Look, you once said a good person should help others improve

---

⁶ Adomas Mickevicius, Velines, Vilnius, 1958, p. 100–101. Translated by Justinas Marcindevicius.

themselves, like the strong need to hold up the weak. Those were your own words. Now, it comes out that a good woman should drive away any admirer and withdraw all contact with him the minute there's some hint that respect could grow into love."

I have no idea what they're talking about, thought Julija listening to the conversation.

"Well I see it completely differently," answered Elvyra. "I'm saying if you choose the wrong person to love, you have to accept that your affection can't grow. Otherwise, you condemn yourself to a sad misery, especially if the object of your infatuation doesn't want to stoop to your level, get involved in a lie or have to cruelly cut off the limited relationship. And if somebody succeeds in seducing his intended, doing that will make his own love dissolve like a bubble of soap.

"I'm not talking about savages from the recent past. These are people who live in our society and who exploit and spoil it with no conscience. They're like parasites with no ties to society – no sense of belonging to it. Society tries to get rid of them like harmful elements. It's enough for them to satisfy their lowest needs in order to be happy – they're like animals. Since they're in a hostile environment, they constantly have feelings that don't lead to happiness."

"What have you done to Mykolas? He looks like he just lost his last bet gambling in Monte Carlo," joked Steponas, entering at the end of peak of the conversation. He wanted to invite everyone to the garden to eat cherries. "Did the Zurich philosopher just bite Mykolas' goat horns?"

Julija's cheeks flushed.

"I'm sorry," she said. "Mr. Mykolas was having a talk with Auntie and since they didn't agree, he's understandably upset."

"Oh, but my dear, you're blushing like a berry," Steponas kidded Julija. Seeing that she was near tears, he changed the subject.

"Let's go eat cherries. They were just picked. Enough to make the room groan!"

Then he suggested to the guests:

"You know, Mykolas, nothing is going to come of your peat business. I got a letter from Mruvcinski. He says our climate is too humid to dry peat in the open air. And to dry it in another way, the production costs are too high and not profitable. He's pretty accurate about these things."

"How does this Mruvcinski know all that much?" Mykolas rashly mumbled. "He just wants to see great profit and doesn't have any capital. It's a rare business that's profitable to the point that the interest on a loan is covered and you net something beyond that. I'd be satisfied to get just a small percentage from my investment, just enough to have an income and some assurance that my work is an asset to the region. I also find it motivating that there are people nearby whose example gives me strength and inspiration."

Steponas intently looked at him, and then at his wife. Elvyra understood his look. A second passed. She felt cold, as if her husband had exposed something she'd done wrong. Because of her discomfort, she looked down and hung her head in defense. Steponas saw her involuntary reaction. Eyes blazing with anger he turned on Mykolas, his face full of irritation and rage.

"In other words, it seems, your interest is mainly 'to benefit society.' But we all thought you were after nothing more than profit. If you have other reasons..."

"No! Again, Steponas! You sound as if what's most important to you is material gain and that you don't pay any heed to the community you work with. As for me, it's here with you that I feel most comfortable, more than anywhere else, and I won't hide the fact that I want to live and work near you. I'm sure if I returned to Warsaw, I'd be overcome with apathy again and wouldn't have the energy to work the way I did before I came to Egliai."

Elvyra struggled with the cold feeling that took over due to Steponas' suspicions. What a strange intersection: when someone looks at us with clear blame and we know it, and we feel against our will as if that blame were justified. Hoping to correct the impression, she raised her head and looked Steponas in the eye as she normally did, assertively and sincerely, indicating that his doubts were unfounded. She felt much better.

Right then Julija agreed with Mykolas:

"I agree with you, Mykolas: it's always better to be poor among good and close friends rather than make millions among strangers and people you don't like."

Julija's words encouraged Mykolas. He felt very grateful to her and sincerely thanked her for her kindness and support.

Storm

Although the storm soon subsided, clouds still darkened the horizon at Egliai. From time to time some kind of shadow of worry passed over Steponas' brow, his male ego was constantly searing and the need to be vigilant bothered him a lot. It seemed to Steponas that Mykolas had become tiresome and everyone felt it. Increasingly he spoke badly of him to his wife, and when Elvyra tried to defend Mykolas, he become exasperated, cold, saying she didn't understand people, kept changing her mind, and still a thousand other unspoken things.

Elvyra figured that Steponas was gnawing on jealousy and tried to avoid anything that would disturb his mood. It was still fresh in her mind that she herself had endured this feeling and for that reason she was sympathetic. She was determined to make every effort to keep Mykolas from staying in the area. What would their lives be like? Steponas was still very upset, and their marriage would deteriorate. Mykolas was still a zealous, discordant hanger-on. It seemed they would all three go on in conflict, secretly, until they ran out of energy, and soon they'd start to argue and other disagreeable things. They needed to take strict measures as soon as possible and stop Mykolas from staying there once and for all.

It's too bad, she thought, *that Mykolas doesn't understand me. He's practically blind, that's all. Before, I thought of him with a sympathetic woman's heart and acted as if all roads were open for him, and were waiting for him. You can meet people like Mykolas often among decadents – he's apathetic, bored, doesn't want anything and isn't interested in anything. Furthermore, it seems to him that under my wing he came alive. Isn't he really like a child who thinks he can walk when his mother is holding his hand, and the minute he's left to walk on his own, he falls down? But I didn't lead him by the hand! Isn't it interesting what gives him pleasure in life?*

She imagined Mykolas returning to Warsaw. Rejected by her, incapable of looking at life critically, and feeling that he was abused. That he was robbed of love. Distressed, worthless. People tormented him and he'd had enough. Life was becoming exasperating and eventually he threw himself into everything that seemed to make him feel alive – alcohol, playing cards...

A few days passed after Mykolas bluntly told Steponas about his reckless interest in starting a peat business. During that time Elvyra avoided him a bit at a time. She wanted to think about the best way, what and how she needed to tell him, encouraging him to go away from their district. Whereas Mykolas made sure that in time nothing would prevent him from living here. Soon he started to make arrangements, writing letters, making plans. This took up a lot of time, leaving him less time to spend with Elvyra.

Steponas' mood did not get better. Often when he returned to the manor house, he roughly shouted at one of the servants, yelled at the children, and was surly with Elvyra. He stayed away from the direct presence of Mykolas. When he talked to him, he was never animated, remaining cool and polite. Mykolas, immersed in his own activities, didn't even notice this disinterest in being with him. The farm workers noticed Steponas' remoteness. They'd never been bothered before.

"Do you have a problem?" they asked Steponas as he sat back silent and glum, tapping his fingers on the table. "Is there some way I can help you?"

"It's okay," Steponas would say, coming around. "I have to go into town today, because I never got an answer to a telegram, on an urgent matter."

Saying that he stood up and went to look for people to let them know he was leaving. Then he had a very early tea. After tea Steponas got his things and left. The town he was going to was about one kilometer away. Because he had to meet up with his lawyer the next day, he would only get back to Egliai the next night.

Elvyra decided to finish all her work for the day in order to free up the next day from early morning, when she could go out to the fields, oversee the threshing of rye, plowing of fields, and also, drive around with the steward to various grounds. Julija asked Mykolas and Vytautas to play croquet because it was a beautiful evening and nice outside. To have four players Julija invited Jasius, got the balls, wickets, and mallets and took them all to the lawn where they usually played croquet.

It was a July evening, warm and quiet. A few frogs were croaking, a chorus of grasshoppers in answer, and in the bushes fireflies glowed their phosphorus-like flashlights. The game started. Julija, waiting her turn, sat down on a grassy knoll. Maryte, Vytukas and Adomelis brought her some dragonflies, a luminous little bug. Julija put it on her hair. After a bit, it lit up again and framed the girl's forehead with a tiara. The children thought it was awesome. They were

111

excited to show this wonderful thing to their mother. They dashed home and pestered Elvyra until she agreed to come and look at the amazing thing. Dusk came over the lawn. If it wasn't for moonlight shining over the croquet court, they couldn't keep playing.

"A wreath of bugs looks good on you," she said, approaching Julija. "And what a beautiful day! I'm jealous that you can play this evening. I still have a lot to do, and need to get back to the house right away."

"Is there anything I can do to help?" Mykolas asked.

"Thanks, but there's nothing that you can help me with...."

"Jasius beat Mykolas!" suddenly Julija turned. "You're out of the game. And that means our team is losing! If Vytautas hits my ball far out right now, without your help we are really going to lose."

"I think the young lady has no reason to worry and we're going to win this round. Just hit it lightly, but firmly, like this..." Mykolas showed her how to hit the ball properly. In his heart, he was quite happy to be out of the game, as it was a chance to talk to Elvyra.

Now the children came running up to decorate her head with a crown of glow worms, forming a halo on her brow. *A real princess!* thought Mykolas, enjoying the sight.

We tend to be bolder in the dark. We think if we're going to lose, nobody's going to notice. Mykolas was emboldened by the magical night. Seeing the children run off to collect more bugs, and Julija arguing with Vytautas and Jasius about some illegal action, he said:

"You look like a holy icon. That's what the halo of bugs the kids put on your head looks like to me."

Elvyra was quiet. Mykolas got even bolder.

"You, my lady, are holy to me without a halo. I admire you like nothing else in the world! Could such respect be of any use? Could it be that you forbid me to live nearby? You're not going to forbid it, are you?... Look, you assured yourself that I'm right in my intention to seek to work in a place where there's good energy, and not a place that's slow."

Elvyra bowed her head and started to gather up the glow-worms, taking them from her head as if she would like to take away the attraction that had such a hold on Mykolas.

"Enough games. We need to... we've got to have a serious talk, Mykolas. We should have some insight, at our age. We need to know how to deal with life. I'm not going to deny the fact that your attention makes me happy. It's a quiet comfort. But I understand the circumstances well enough to question whether you need to leave or stay around here."

She stood up.

"Let's take a walk. I want to talk freely. You have no idea how hard it is for me to talk about this. Surely you remember our conversation when I quoted a passage from 'Old Souls.' It seems to me you haven't understood me at all. And I was thrilled to think that you understood."

"Exactly what did you decide I misunderstood?"

"I don't want to get into an argument. I think we're going to go around in circles. Maybe... maybe you think it's funny. Maybe you'll be hurt if I'm direct. But I'm not used to closing my eyes to something threatening. I want to look it straight in the eye, always." She lifted her head higher. "You're wrong about the nature of your feelings. Maybe it's unconscious. You're giving in to the most common feeling whose aim is to procreate – the normal goal of nature."

"But wait," Mykolas, upset and stunned by her openness.

113

"Please don't think that I say this as a woman with hurt feelings. Not at all! I want the truth, and let's set aside other people who are involved. When we relentlessly seek someone's company, when we can't stop thinking about times we shared and our talks, when the briefest parting feels desolate – that's really being inundated with the instinct to procreate. Although we hope that something more than romantic platonic feelings will show up in another person, it's always a mistake. Because the operative instinct in us is always seeking a goal, and the more it meets obstacles, the more it burns looking for another path to find pure intimacy, commitment and more.

"Let's compare these feelings with those we enjoy in other people close to us, for example, a brother or a sister, for that matter. We love them fairly deeply, but do we think of them every minute? Do we have a passion for them as if we couldn't live without them? Surely not. That's why, when these feelings consume us, even though we think they're noble, do we have a right to stir them up?"

It got completely dark. They stopped playing croquet and gathered on the veranda. Mrs. Songailiene wasn't there anymore. Vytautas excused himself and went to his room. Julija took the children to bed. They were alone again. Elvyra sat in a dark corner away from the light over the dining table. Mykolas stood leaning on a post in the veranda.

"Haven't you gone too far making physical love into a generalized natural kind of love?" he asked. "I won't deny that they have common roots, but they arise in very different circumstances. The way flowers are different when they grow in a shady hollow away from the sun and precious warmth, or how another is a creeper always underfoot and winding around, or another is randomly white as a wall of snow. The same way, feelings of love can be different when they stir in someone's soul, although they start out the same way!"

"Mykolas, you're talking poetry and I'm talking reality. In my opinion, the differentiation of desire from the feeling of love arises only given its evolutionary stage. Do you remember when I gave you an example from the natural world – regarding two males? Maybe it's too stark, but it clearly explains needs: one of the males wants to procreate, and the other doesn't.

"We can divide the male gender into the same categories. For some, love is needed simply to satisfy bodily functions. They can give their love to any woman, with no commitment and no possession. Others surround their chosen one with support and attention, instinctively laying the foundation for their home. For them, their instinctive concern comes from wanting a nurturing mother for prospective progeny, the right environment for their progeny to thrive. They can't fall in love with just any woman. Unconsciously they want to make their family better, to make it strong in the struggle to survive. The right kind of love in nature leads to perfecting the species: that's why we're careful in choosing a partner. When we act on that kind of love, we automatically look for a spouse, who has the ability to take on the work of raising children."

"And why don't you divide women into similar groups?" Mykolas asked.

"Women by nature were given the greatest and most important role – to have children. I regard those who are always looking for new admirers – flirting coquettes – disgraceful human beings. But please pay attention! A man who feels a strong drive to procreate always fights for his family, even if he needs to use primitive methods that are characteristic of lower organisms, although they might be the only reliable means of preserving the species.

"I know women who've felt an attraction, and then use their wits to draw an admirer to themselves, against their better nature. For them, it goes without saying, reproduction isn't important – since they're already women! That kind of perversion does fit the animal world – unless among domesticated animals, but they don't factor in, because they've been corrupted living with humans.

"Just like we like to play at war, we're also very happy to chase after stimulation, and we could control that freedom in ways to keep it from ruining our society. We drink wine and other intoxicants, gamble with cards and put bets on horse races, we flirt – all tempting us as a way to excite masculine energy. But then what should be a means to an end becomes the end itself. Sometimes, when energy surges it could inspire the pursuit of higher things, but we make the means into the end. And with every step we trample the rules of nature, undermining the harmony of society, of humanity, defiling the noble calling of humans."

Elvyra spoke with passion, breathlessly, her voice somewhat shaky, releasing nervous energy. The cumulation of a lifetime of arguments was stirred up. Her exceptional good memory recovered a great deal of material, crowding her mind. She lost her train of thought and felt incredibly tired. If she could explain it to Mykolas without making it about her, she would've been able to speak with more composure. But now she had to focus her mind and suppress her usual reserve.

They sat quiet for a while. The feelings wrestling in Mykolas' psyche were extremely conflicted. He felt unbalanced. He felt a foreboding pressure that he wasn't meant to stay here. Also, he was stunned by Elvyra's words. They were unbelievable, pure candor. The intensity of her passion was puzzling to Mykolas. However, in another minute he got another idea, maybe a hope that doesn't leave us even when something makes us very nervous.

"I'm busting my head," he said, "trying to figure out which of your categories fits me, but in truth I don't think I fit either one. It seems I'm an exception. I've never planned to have a family and didn't feel motivated that way. And I've always been selective in pursuing love, and superficial beauty isn't attractive to me. I mean, I'm never going to agonize about an attachment to family and I won't establish a family. Maybe I have a different destiny. Maybe I'm supposed to contribute in other ways.

"Otherwise, we should think that all people who are childless are parasites, and that's not so. Until I got to know you, I was a sponger. I failed get over my apathy; I lacked purpose and had no adversity. Just as you rightfully called them, my pitiful little articles – written more out of emptiness than any meaningful role. I wasn't giving people anything they needed. You could say that I haven't fully grown up, because I didn't suffer adversity, haven't had any accountable training and don't have a healthy sense of purpose. But I know in advance," he said heatedly, "that when I'm far away from here, the apathy will take over again and when I'm overwhelmed by it, I might not notice that I'm a useless pawn in the arena of life."

"You may think so, but it's not going to happen," Elvyra said, vehemently objecting. "Don't scare yourself, or me! You'll find enough motivation to work. You'll forget the feeling that there's plenty of time and breathing room. A flood of new feelings often creates a false impression that time and space aren't limiting, or that our feelings will go on for an extremely long time and into endless space. But a loss – the death of a loved one – shows us very well that in a moment our feelings can change; they pivot to lifeless memories.

"I wish your conscious 'I' would figure out where your unconscious 'I' is going, and that the latter be more adamant about using a better tool – space or time. I wish that you and I, together, would figure out what would work for both of us and for other people.

"I love Steponas, but that doesn't in the least mean that I have to give up my voice in having certain emotions. It doesn't mean that the expression of honest feelings from other people can't elicit a response from me in return. When somebody tells me they hurt, I know they feel hurt. I'm used to helping people who are suffering and when I hear them cry out, I come running to help. That's the way it is with all our experiences and feelings.

"Let's say someone is getting his foot amputated. I hear him moan. My conscious 'I' tells me to drop the idea that I should run to help them, because in this case it's not needed. Still, the moaning tears my heart a lot and I want to run far away from it, so I won't hear it. And why is it hard to hear crying, when I know it means he's getting healed? Because, the irrational part of me doesn't understand and responds as if the pain was a sign of danger."

Mykolas was disheartened. Elvyra's way of thinking took away grounds for any hope, even the tiniest, or the furthest.

"I'm leaving," he said suddenly, his voice weak. "I won't bother you. I still strongly disagree that any 'amputation' is necessary."

Elvyra saw that she'd hurt Mykolas' ego.

"Mykolas, I know you're mad, and maybe you blame my selfishness. But here's what I suggest... Trust me, I honestly wish you good luck. I'm not sorry you came here. Mykolas," she said, putting out her hand, "I know I can't convince you, but listen: please postpone the peat business for a year. Okay?" she asked, squeezing his hand. "Okay? You'll leave for a year, won't you?"

Mykolas started to kiss her hand sensually and she abruptly pulled it away. "You can come and visit after a year, and..." She laughed all of a sudden. "You'll tell us that you've gotten married. And we'll be very happy, delighted for you. You'll see... And all that's happened today will be just a pleasant memory. We won't let the situation control us; we'll take charge. It's late. Good-night."

She gave him her hand. Mykolas put it to his lips and kissed it several times again.

"Just one more word," he said. "I wouldn't be honest if I didn't confess that I appreciate your idealism. But I can't deny that I get some vague optimism from your words. What'll come of it? I don't know today. From the moment I saw you, my mind was thrown into chaos. I didn't have time to integrate a new way of thinking that was quite different from the usual path my mind walked.

"I'd lost, as you say, 'a purpose in life.' I believe in you and your kindness. And for the time being, that's enough for me. There's just one thing that I can't accept: that I should give up my plan to work with local peat. To be honest, I don't understand why you're fixed in your opinion – why you're adamant – that I need to hold off on this plan for a year. I hope that I'll succeed in carrying out my plan, and not in opposition to your opinion. Or even my own. Good-night."

119

Doubts

They parted.

In his room, Mykolas dropped into an armchair, put his hands to his head and mulled things over. He'd moved himself away from the laid-back salon atmosphere of Warsaw to here, where the environment was completely different. There was hard work to be done, a hearty active community and work that was important to society. They spoke plainly and thought straight. Here he was, a darling of Warsaw salons, famous for telling jokes and behaving badly. He, the unspoken champion of his group who could arrange parties whose description could make his friends sigh with wonder. He, who had always been spoiled with success, completely lost the ground under his feet his first minute in Egliai.

Here he was but a lowly resident, who had climbed higher in some other place. The wind blows on wintry hills, lashing his chest until it hurts, allowing him to feel, sometimes, a greater power over the constraints of his birth, over his ideas and his boldest ambitions. These strange aspirations of his soul in excess were crushed, beaten down by their own weight. From this height, his earlier life – the old struggles, successes, worries, sorrows, drunken binges, orgies – looked quite pitiful and he couldn't stand his shame, his supreme wretchedness.

Finally, the time came to react. Although he wanted to forget the unproductive feelings, Mykolas started to mock them, to torment himself.

I was too quick to be enthusiastic, he thought. *I let myself picture myself in the bucolic countryside. Her request that I spend a year in suspension – it's just an excuse more appropriate to a child. 'If you still don't understand that it would be good for you, then do it for Mommy,' they say to a naughty boy.*

Everything he didn't get until now suddenly came clear to him. Steponas' constant sour face, his rude behavior toward him – various episodes morphed into a panoramic view. He was fuming. Then ashamed. How could it have been hard to see, when he'd spent a long time out here? How could he not see it – he, who was usually super insightful! What made him blind! 'Bad direction' – a fragment from Elvyra's words. Sure, a bad direction!

Suddenly it struck him that, really, nothing ever comes of caring only for himself, always himself. He never suffered for other people. *What am I upset about?* he asked himself. *Why am I strongly attracted to her? Why do I think about her all the time?*

Exhausted, but still finding no answer, he lay down on the bed. He drew an improbable scene in his mind. Elvyra, in love with him, struggles with her feelings of responsibility, but she can't suppress her love. He makes her swoon every day with his heated passion. They stroll through the garden feeling a thousand times wonderful. In the end, Elvyra is worn down. She can't resist, she gives herself up…

His head flushed with blood. He collected himself and immediately got the awful feeling that he'd just put Elvyra in with the same company as most other women who'd always submitted to him, sooner or later, easily or with some trouble. For a long time, he couldn't purge this ugly feeling.

He fell asleep only at daybreak.

A bewildered Julija surprised Elvyra in her bedroom. She couldn't get over her distress and her worry. *Why was Auntie against Mykolas' plan to start a peat business? What are they talking about all the time?* She searched in vain for answers to these questions.

"Dear Auntie," she asked as soon as Elvyra entered the room. "Please don't be mad, but I…" She didn't know how to begin. "Auntie, I'm really interested to know. I don't understand at all, why you're against Mykolas' work with peat."

She blushed. It was obvious she was upset and if she could, she'd take back what she just said.

"My child," Elvyra said when she stopped talking. "I'm glad you trust with me your questions. Otherwise you wouldn't ask. If you didn't trust me you'd have chosen to think that I can get out of giving you an honest answer. Believe me, Julija, I only want the best for Mykolas, and although right now I can't explain why I act the way I have toward him, to you, believe me, nothing bad is going to come of it. To anyone," she repeated again and gave Julija a kiss.

Julija hugged her and kissed her hand warmly, in spite of her objection.

Crisis

When Mykolas came for tea in the morning, Elvyra was already gone. Working out on the farm, she was taking care of tasks that Steponas had left for her. For the first time the coffee was served in the dining room, because it was rainy and windy outside. Julija served, assuming the role of the hostess of the house. However, once in a while she put her hand to her head while her thoughts drifted far, far away. Mykolas briefly glanced at Julija from time to time and noticed her unusual distraction, and noticed also that she was much paler than usual, which made her all the more comely. When he got up for his second cup of coffee, he didn't return to his seat but sat next to Julija instead. She was obviously pleased and quite affectionately offered him cake, sugar, and sour cream.

"You seem to be off in your mind. May I ask what you're thinking about?"

Julija looked askew at Mykolas, not turning her head.

"Too bad I have to go back to awful Zurich soon. Sad to leave a beautiful summer on the farm!..."

"I feel the same way. I don't want to go back to Warsaw at all."

"But did you abandon your plan to start a peat factory around here?" Julija nimbly asked.

"Yes, I dropped it. Instead I decided not to rush into it, think about the idea more thoroughly in theory. It may be better to start this business abroad. I haven't completely decided. And when are you leaving?" He was suddenly interested.

Julija again felt her heart beat faster, and, spoke even more wanting to hide her nerves, spoke even more slowly. The grave tone suited her very well.

"I'm going back to my parents' in a week. In three weeks, I'll be in Warsaw, where I have an uncle and aunt whom I want to visit. After that I'm off to Vienna and Switzerland."

"You mean you're going to be in Warsaw!" Mykolas turned with honest delight. "May I know the uncle's name?"

"Janas Danilovicius."

"Janas Danilovicius! I know him. I've visited your aunt and uncle. Steponas took me there some time ago. Very friendly home. Your aunt is a tremendous singer. She was quite beautiful in her youth."

"She's beautiful to me now."

"I don't deny that. But if she were younger, she'd be even more beautiful. You have luck with beautiful aunts! I'm thinking of Elvyra."

Julija was offended by Mykolas' teasing tone. She didn't hide her dismay. But Mykolas went on making fun.

"Oh my, I forgot. Not allowed to talk about these things with the Queen of the Uzventis Ball. But you'll excuse my being this blunt, won't you?"

Anger loomed on Julija's face.

"Isn't it too early for you, at your age, to make sarcastic jokes and take liberties?" she answered, unable to stand his patronizing tone.

Such cheek didn't put off Mykolas. Quite the opposite, it made him respect her more.

126

"I see that I've hurt you with my wicked words," he said with gravity, careless in his pretense, which was especially annoying to Julija. "Please forgive me. I definitely want to leave Egliai with no bad thoughts about me."

"I really like Egliai too," Julija said now lighter. "It's beautiful here... The surroundings are quiet and spiritually harmonizing! Maybe because everyone is soulful, everyone's appreciated. Even the regular house servants work at the highest standard. Everyone works together as if they were partners, each properly doing the job assigned to him."

"I'm guessing it's because of Elvyra's management," Mykolas said without hesitation.

Julija jumped to defend her uncle, thinking of many times when he was strategic in his interactions with people, winning them to his side. Not everyone was able to make casual conversation and motivate workers to their jobs.

Soon the whole company gathered in the living room. It was raining outside, pounding on the roof and the windows.

"Poor Steponas is going to be soaked to the skin. I don't remember if they took an umbrella," sighed Elvyra.

"They'll buy one if they're in town," reassured Songailiene, wrapped in a shawl that Julija helpfully brought her.

"I'm leaving. Egliai lost its charming, sunny spirit," said Mykolas, sadly.

"Are you leaving?" Songailiene asked, surprised. "Weren't you going to work with peat in this area?"

"I planned to. But nobody's too excited about my interest... Besides, I haven't thought through a business like that, enough that I'd start working right away."

So, I convinced him, thought Elvyra. *He listened to me and he's leaving.* She looked at Mykolas. He didn't look like a man who was disappointed. He wasn't in the least depressed. When she noticed that, Elvyra got worried that his feelings about every decision was affected by her influence. Persuading someone that our concern for somebody else was much more important that his distress couldn't be pleasant. But Elvyra was… a woman. She was happy that he was going do what she thought he should do. But she couldn't believe the turning point happened to him with no effort or distress. It had to hurt. And why did he seem happy again? What brought him around? Was it Julija? At that thought Elvyra got more friendly. The frustration in her selfish nature disappeared without a trace.

After short silence Mykolas asked:

"Do you know Nietzsche?"

"I know him, but I'm not a big fan. Nietzsche thinks if you trample the weak, you'll free yourself and cleanse yourself of weakness. It seems to me he's quite wrong. It's not true that the most powerful are those who are afraid of losing their power. The minute humankind started to take care of its weaker members, it found strength in a collective struggle for survival, because they want to live giving both the strong and the weak a chance.

"Among people, only those who are really strong are those who want to give others strength. And the weak don't find any other way to have influence except to weaken their own environment. Maybe because of that the weak hate it when you brag about something to them and they themselves fail to say anything good to anyone. An egotist is the weakest person of all, because he wants everything for himself, and doesn't give anything to anyone in return."

"Different paths lead to the same end," added Mykolas.

"Namely: *jede Kraft hat ihre Gegenkraft*[7]," answered Elvyra. "Everything in the world for some reason doesn't take the shortest route, the easiest route, but twists and turns around. That's the only way we can explain the advantage of a society that gives us thinkers like Nietzsche and an abundant line of followers after him.

"Sometimes we watch pounding waves at the beach, and we wonder how they're formed: in the wind that mightily strikes the top of the water, which, following the law of gravity, is constantly trying to flatten out again, and that causes swells. Just as the wind can't push the water from the bottom of the sea – because the force of gravity is stronger there than the wind – the same way, a wind like Nietzsche and his followers doesn't raise anything in the sea of human life, aside from the waves on the surface. There are some innocent creatures scattered about like rocks against which the waves break and splatter. But the universal aspiration in human nature is to seek your own channel.

"Some are super smart and uncritically chase after a genius who speaks of goodness and truth, having a real goal. They reach a certain level that they might ask: 'What is goodness? What is truth? What is great? What is small?' And we have to admit – they're taking a big step forward. Think of the way Newton needed an extraordinary faculty in order to raise questions, after observing such a simple fact that an apple falls from a tree to the ground. He had to find the faculty in himself to critique his own thinking. Newton did

---

[7] Every force has its opposite force

not discover gravity, he just confirmed it, that is to say he helped us realize it.

"Nature pushes toward eternity and we can't throw off that force without a lot of trouble. Conversely, our success depends on cooperating with that natural force. Unless it stops halfway. For example, when we ask what's good and evil and we look for criteria for each one, and then we don't find any. Nietzsche came to the wrong conclusion, that there is no such thing as good and evil.

"In my opinion, the essence of goodness is when we succeed in living, and conversely, evil is when life doesn't turn out. That means goodness is relative, because if one person wins in the struggle for survival, then it's always at the expense of others. Regarding the conscious reproduction of all the human race, goodness grows when it helps someone, even if it constrains the freedom of a single individual and limits his attempt to sow more seeds. Because goodness is a state of our emotional development, a development in life and in emotional attitude, then, if someone at some time was good to us, we can disregard it.

"For example, in prehistoric times the best man was someone who was physically strong and could kill the enemy most often. When civilization got more refined, the best man became someone who was able to be nice and act humanely toward his enemies. In both times, being good is useful to a real group of people. Only our concept of goodness, and how it's applied, changes.

"The same principle helps us understand the idea of 'beauty' also. Beauty – it's feeling a certain wish. Just like goodness it's a certain point of view. Beauty – it's the same as goodness, only in the domain of our feelings, feelings that are unconscious and that are hard to comprehend, because we don't know under what circumstances it is true forever and ever and what experiences or feelings prompt us to see it."

The conversation on the porch was suspended on the sound of wheels rattling. Elvyra and the others after her left the porch to greet the waiting Steponas. But the carriage was empty. She asked the driver "Where's the gentleman?" but he didn't answer. He slowly unbuttoned a drenched woolen overcoat and pulled a wrinkled letter from his chest. Her hands shaking with impatience, Elvyra took the envelope and ripped it open.

"It's not from Steponas," she said, shocked. "Oh my. It's from Susevskis!"

She read the letter quickly and went pale. The hand holding the letter went limp.

The letter said: "My dear Lady, today your husband's wagon overturned on its way back home, and he broke his leg. A motorcar made the horse bolt and caused the accident. His life is not in danger. He was brought to my house, injured, and immediately I gave him some medicine to help. He eagerly asks that you please send a carriage tomorrow and you can bring the patient home."

Elvyra decided to go to her husband right away. In a few minutes, she was ready to leave. Impatient for the carriage to pull up she wanted to run to the stables and urge them to harness the horses faster. Mykolas hurried after her to help. Seeing her agitation, he tried to calm her down. Elvyra was too distracted to listen, thinking only about Steponas, and about how she wanted to bring him back to Egliai and what she might need at the moment. Now and then she gave instructions to the servants: bring a lap blanket, a pillow, some item of clothing. Anupras who'd been invited to tea that evening, requested a horse be harnessed for him, intending to accompany Elvyra.

"Maybe I can help someway, in town," he said.

"Maybe I can help out too," added Mykolas. "If it's all right with you. I'd be happy to ride in the wagon with you. I don't want to get in the way. I know when something bad happens, a stranger can be a bother."

Anupras graciously agreed to take him. Soon both the teams pulled up to the veranda. Elvyra got in the carriage and took off first. The two men were in a wagon behind her.

Alone in the carriage, Elvyra breathed easier. Her hands and feet were trembling from the rush, and painful spasms ran through her back. Two hours' journey separated her from Steponas. *Two long hours! Was he in terrible pain? Was he waiting for her? Is he going meet her with distrust at the outset and say something harsh?... Will he appreciate her rushing to him in a deluge of emotion?... Maybe he still suspects her of having too much sympathy for Mykolas? It must be hard for him! Hurry to him!* Although the horses galloped like the wind, she leaned forward trying to lengthen their gait. She took comfort that she'd declared all her love to him. She wanted to reassure him that he wouldn't suffer for nothing. This was a year in which her stormiest feelings came out. Now she rushed with all her heart.

She remembered a terrible time when she was sick with typhus, and Steponas, barely out of the greatest danger himself, risked going into N. town to buy medicine. Oh! Even now her heart aches! Life seemed awful. Death from typhus, like a release from misery... She was forced to go on living for fear that the care of her children would pass on to some awful woman. Yes, only due to that fear did she take the medicine she was pressured to take. Worry about the children was a stronger motivation than the instinct for self-preservation. She was her own living example that in nature, concern for the species trumps concern for the individual.

Again, her thoughts went back to Steponas. It was still about six kilometers to town. That meant she would see him in half an hour and ease her deepest worry. Suddenly she remembered that behind her rode Mykolas with Anupras. She felt maybe the wrong notes were playing in her heart. It wasn't nice that Mykolas' sense of duty and sympathy might be greeted with rudeness – but Steponas probably will not want to see Mykolas. *I can't bring him there*, she thought. *But tomorrow, I think, Steponas' suspicions will be dismissed forever!...*

Finally, she arrived at the house of the lawyer Susevskis. Anupras and Mykolas rushed to help her out of the carriage.

"Thank you for your kindness. You'll be staying in the Hamburg Hotel. Please have my horses put up there. You'll probably want to visit Steponas tomorrow. We'll expect you. Again, I'm very grateful. Good night!..." she said.

However, Elvyra didn't manage to send them away until a servant came. Both men protested, not happy to leave her at the locked door. They left only when the servant brought her luggage in and closed the door after Elvyra.

Soon a doctor entered the living room.

"Your husband isn't sleeping. He heard the clatter of the carriage and the wagon with the men and asked what happened. He broke his leg at the knee. I managed to brace it and bind it. We put an ice compress on it to ease the pain. The patient is clearly better but he still can't sleep. That's understandable," he added quickly, seeing that Elvyra was worried. "He was very happy when I told him you were here.

Come this way..." he said and led her into the room where Steponas lay.

He looked drained and sallow in the dim light. Even though the doctor was there, Elvyra burst into tears on greeting him.

"Who came with you?" Steponas asked in a voice stressed with pain.

Elvyra hesitated.

"Anupras was visiting us at Egliai, waiting for you. We came over together. He'll visit tomorrow for sure... I think he'll be able to stand in for you, watching over the patient," she said, turning to the doctor.

"That's fine. You don't really need me anymore. I'd just like to warn you that it's best if the patient is moved as little as possible. The compress needs to be changed at least every hour. Good night."

After the doctor left, Elvyra kneeled beside her husband, took his hand, put it to her warm cheek. Steponas felt her tears fall on his hand.

"Why are you crying?" he asked. "You can't think my life's in danger?"

"Steponuk!" She turned to him. "How could you even think it! I'm crying because I'm sad that you have to suffer. I feel for you. I don't know what to do to make you feel better."

"Really?!"

There was a tone and a wonder in his question, as if what he'd heard was astounding to him and brought back the pleasure of happy memories, and warmth, and gratitude. With this one word, he wanted to reward Elvyra for the feelings she expressed unexpectedly.

Elvyra hadn't heard anything like this from him in a long time. She herself hadn't spoken from her heart with him.

A fight had broken out between them since she'd gotten to know Mykolas. When Steponas started to feel suspicious and angry about Mykolas' imposition toward her, he became cool and aloof, in a bad mood. Mykolas' deference to her helped her feel better about herself, and she stopped trying to compete for Steponas' attention. She didn't even seek it any more. They parted ways and neither tried to rekindle their prior intimacy. Little by little they turned down a path where the value on intimacy and harmony in the marriage faded from sight. An accident opened their eyes – as is often the case.

Bedridden and cramped with pain, Steponas understood what Elvyra meant to him maybe for the first time in his life. Now all her good qualities came to life in front of him: whatever his fate he could trust her; trust that she wouldn't leave him, wouldn't deceive him or betray him; trust that when he saw that she was unhappy he would try even harder to wrap her in caring and love; and finally, he could be certain that his children would be raised well even if he were gone and the standard he set for them would never be compromised. *It's a great blessing to be able to trust your wife,* he thought, looking at Elvyra. His eyes lit up with joy.

"Are you feeling a little better?" she asked, concerned, noticing his lighter expression.

"My heart is better having you here," he answered. "I'm just worried that you're going to get too tired here with me."

"My goodness, don't make up a new problem, thinking that I'm anything but fine! Do you think I could sleep at home right now? I'm glad I didn't wait until tomorrow. It's nice that you feel better having me here!"

Steponas stroked her hand.

"My dear! My love!" he whispered sweetly, leaning toward her.

Steponas, trying to lean over and hug her, moved his foot and cried out in pain. Elvyra jumped away with alarm.

"Oh! I'm careless and clumsy!" she turned, ashamed. "Don't move! For God's sake, lie still. Should I change the compress?... Just be still!"

Soon the pain eased up, and Steponas calmed down and fell asleep. Elvyra's presence was very soothing. She stayed quiet about an hour and then felt very sleepy herself. She closed her eyes and dozed off in the armchair. However, pain didn't let Steponas sleep very long. Barely feeling a little stronger, he opened his eyes. Elvyra slept on.

Steponas watched his wife with warmth. *She's such a good wife*, he thought. *She dropped everything and came! Worried about me as if I were the best husband. What a jerk I was, walking all over her feelings! But is that why I've been cold? At the time, I couldn't think or feel any other way. I'm not blaming myself.* And yet something still bothered him. *What is it?* he asked himself.

We can feel sympathy for something not just in the present but also in the past and in the future. We're able to understand that someone has suffered, been hit with adversity, that's how we can feel sympathy and realize that someone has suffered because of a hardship in the past. Steponas just now felt insight into his wife's pain before and just now understood how important it was. Why? Perhaps because he himself hadn't felt jealous in a long time, and now she was responding to Mykolas.

He couldn't fault her for her conduct. Lately life was becoming intolerable to him. Everything made him angry, aggravated, even the children, whom he loved. Work fell from his hands and increased his sense of outrage. He left the house whenever he could. Sometimes he felt like grabbing Mykolas by the throat and throwing him out the door without ceremony. He compared his own groundless suspicions with those that had torn Elvyra's heart, when he himself was the cause, and he was overcome with tremendous pity for his wife.

Poor thing! he thought. *In other words, I shunned her for no good reason. My pride wouldn't let me show the slightest kindness. And sometimes she had to put up with my caresses, with such a wounded heart, when she had no reason to trust my sincerity. Horrible, and cruel! How could I be blind?* A shudder went through him and the pain in his leg came back. He moaned loudly. Elvyra startled awake.

"My goodness, I fell asleep... I'll change your compress. Were you able to sleep a little?"

"I slept, but not very long. I'm glad to see you got some rest, somehow. I tried to suffer in silence as long as I could. I didn't want to wake you."

Elvyra couldn't stop being amazed at Steponas' thoughtfulness. Before, he was quite lacking in sympathy and even very rude. *It seems that suffering has taught him this feeling,* she thought. *A harsh teacher.*

Steponas suffered into the morning. The pain never let up. Elvyra also never closed her eyes – she tried to ease his condition as much as possible. At daybreak, she requested that the doctor be called back because things got worse for Steponas.

Anupras and Mykolas arrived with the doctor. They wanted to know how Steponas was doing and was there anything they could do. Elvyra went out to greet them. The night had changed her and made her strange. Her pretty face was haggard, dark circles surrounded her eyes, and her lips, clamped together tightly, showed her heartache. She put her hand out to each man in greeting and looking at the doctor, said:

"My husband is in pain all the time. Is there anything that'll reduce the pain? Also, he has a high fever. Is that a bad complication?"

The doctor's face took on a sad, meaningful expression. He patted his ample chest, raised his eyebrows, cast a look into the distance and said to himself:

"Hmm... It was a very hard blow. I'll have to recommend something. The fever will go down... He's not sleeping, there's nausea – that's understandable. If the cold compresses don't help, we'll try heat – maybe that's better? Other than that, I want to examine him."

"Do you think we need to call someone else for a consultation?" asked Elvyra, annoyed with his indecision.

"I have nothing against it, if that's what you want," he spoke casually, "Allow me to examine him."

He nodded and hurried off to Steponas' room with calm and dignity. Elvyra behind him.

Anupras and Mykolas were silent as they discreetly listened to the exchange.

To Mykolas, Elvyra looked like an entirely different woman in the serious situation where she was single-minded and focused with all her heart, under a halo of disaster. He had even more sympathy and respect for her in distress. Now he didn't want to think about those feelings that were aroused in him before. The passion with which he pursued her was ugly. Everything that he'd felt for her until then seemed despicable, low-class, bad, inappropriate!

How could I have been wrong, and failed to appreciate this woman?! She felt it, she knew it, and she even told me so. She tried to turn me to the right path, shielding herself from my love, avoiding shame. And I was relentless, like a fool incapable of feeling the soul's highest desire, after a soul stabbed with pain having known the sins of humanity, who heads straight into it with weeping eyes instead of running away afraid of the perpetual insatiability of human passion. Most likely she was repelled because I demeaned her spiritually, tore away her honor.

Not once, not a single minute did I sense any conflict on her side, that her spirit was ground into flour, the feeling that human dignity was crushed. Nothing from her, aside from gentle, honest acceptance. Where did she learn as much as she knows about the human heart, from what ocean did she draw such patience? What gave her the ability to change someone like me? After all, I feel like a different person after today! It took a minute. Although I still don't know my plans or my job, I have no doubt that I won't go wrong if I listen to myself, to the voice of my conscious self, and decide something.

Could an hour like this strike in another place and other circumstance? Did it require that that poor Steponas break his leg, and Zodeika take me along in his wagon, in order for me to know her, in order for me to come here and see her here?! How strange… It is indeed strange that a man is only a toy in the blind hand of fate!

Anupras woke him from his reverie.

"I wanted to advise Mrs. Steponas," he said quietly, in a muted assuring voice, "that she invite a specialist from Warsaw or Petersburg. You can't fool around with things like this!"

They went to the door of the patient's room and knocked. Elvyra came into the living room.

"Will we be able to see Steponas?" asked Anupras.

Worry shadowed Elvyra's face.

"I'll ask him. He's worn out from pain. It's probably unwise to visit with him now. Let's wait until he gets better."

"You're absolutely right," Anupras said. "In fact, why do we need to see him. Our comfort isn't going to make him stronger, and we could wear him out."

"Would you like to send any message to Egliai?" asked Mykolas.

"Oh, thank you. You've reminded me of an important thing. They're sure to be very worried."

She thought for a minute.

"There is no way Steponas can be moved back to Egliai right now. Although it could cheer him up to see the children… It would be good if Julija would bring them one day."

"I can go to Egliai and bring Julija and the children," said Mykolas. "After that I'll hurry straight to Warsaw. If needed, I can try to send a surgeon for Steponas."

In the end, they decided that Anupras would stay with Elvyra and Steponas because they might need him. And Mykolas would take Anupras' wagon to Egliai and from there he'll send it with a message to Anupras' wife. After that he'll rush back to town with other horses, bringing Julija and the children.

New Light

It wasn't but two hours after returning to Egliai that Mykolas was already rattling back on the same route with a chattering bunch. The three youngest children were sitting on the spacious upper bench in front, their backs to the horses, and Jasius had asked his grandmother to let him sit on the coachman's seat. Mykolas and Julija sat on the bench in the cabin, laden with a pile of clothing which they brought for the children in case it got colder. They traveled in silence, from time to time broken by the children yelling in delight when they saw something new. Julija, seriously anxious, chided them when they got too boisterous, while the children gladly listened but at the same time kept on every time. On the other hand, the girl was lost in thought. Sighing with gloom, a frown creased her clear forehead – she was upset about Steponas' accident and Elvyra's distress.

Mykolas didn't try to disturb the quiet: he respected her mood. Still, he was quite pleased to look at Julija, and he needed no other diversion. She was normally pleasant and out-going, and looked even more attractive now with such a serious expression, taking over Elvyra's role while she nursed her husband.

The way she looked, with long eyelashes framing her almond eyes, as she tended to the children, as she expressed her caring and her fear, was completely genuine. She wanted to shower them with care because they were faced with a hard time. Although it made no sense for them to be carefree around her, just delighting in the adventure, not asking questions about the reason for this adventure – her care was helpful and kind, not unhappy and sad.

"Are you cold, Jasius, up there?" Julija asked, noticing that the boy was as red as a crab from the wind. "Do you want to sit inside?"

"No, no! I'm fine. If Grandma let me, then don't worry. I won't get too cold!"

"Nothing's going to happen to him," Mykolas supported Jasius. "The boy's hardy. Anyway, it's not that cold."

"The wind has picked up. Nothing's worse than a cold for a child. I don't want to add to my Aunt's problems. What if one of the children were to get sick now?"

She covered the children, while the wind played strands of her blond hair flying out from a pretty dark green felt hood.

"What a thoughtful companion the children found!"

"Did you see my uncle?" Julija changed the subject.

"No, I didn't see him."

"And my aunt?"

"I saw her. She was quite different. She looked older after the one night."

"Poor thing, my poor aunt! Poor Uncle!" sighed Julija, tears coming to her eyes.

Mykolas was sympathetic. He would be happy to hug this good child, calm her, wipe the tears from those beautiful eyes! He gently took her hand and put it to his lips.

"My heart aches to see your tears. Please don't worry! Maybe, God willing, everything will be all right."

His words had the opposite effect. For a minute, Julija held back but finally couldn't stop herself. Tears as big as peas spilled over her reddened cheeks.

Things got tense. When the children saw her upset they tried to console her and then they started crying. Julija used this to shift attention from her own worry. She started to point out cows grazing in the meadow to the children, to distract them.

"Look how tiny!.. Sweet!... Wonderful!..." she gasped, seeing the frisky baby goats.

Now Julija had mixed feelings: the earlier sadness for the unfortunate accident that happened to her Aunt's family and now, awash with happiness, a thrill in her heart that Mykolas showed such warmth.

Mykolas completely succumbed to her charm. The same Julija whom he had until then seen as a stranger and someone who meant nothing to him now felt close, very, very close.

Mykolas had been in love many times in his life! More exactly, not that he himself loved, but that he allowed himself to be loved. In return, like a gallant gentleman who is sophisticated and responsible, who suffers through another's feelings, until the last minute of gratification, who then with regret says to himself: *C'est plus fort que moi.*[8] He tried to give his Chosen One everything he could offer of his generous nature.

Truth be told, he didn't choose – he was chosen! Among all the women he liked he was careful, even though he embraced them – up until the minute the idyllic longing

---

[8] It's stronger than me.

started to drift into the sphere of clear lust, leaving no doubt as to its conclusion. His memories of gratification and times of frustration gave him wings, and not even once did he break off a relationship in which he expected a bad outcome from the beginning, always running short of nerve.

That's how he protected himself: with an assumed coolness and sometimes irony. The more it gave his personality a kind of allure, the more he attracted women, in whom he condescended to pay attention, cleverly, meeting attacks and even heartbreak with agility. He was like a passenger on a sinking ship forced to accept circumstances and the worst of human nature as a random victim...

That meant that amorous adventures from the very beginning were always ruled by a romanticism, and it was possible to pay attention to that alone and then in a rare moment, wake up as a different person, with the most shameful feelings!... He blamed them for his moral decline, the habit of seeing women as a means of satisfying himself physically.

However, after he met Elvyra, he learned to see women with different eyes. He agonized that a single whisk of a ghost from the past might scare up, that sometimes they could still bother him. But could those bad days significantly change his relationship with Elvyra? Never, no way! "Clinging to hope" Mykolas, just as Elvyra said. He lived with an illusion, until events in the days of the recent past opened his eyes. Until then, dreaming that his fantasy relationship with Elvyra would come to be, he always avoided Steponas. It didn't even occur to him that a third person could somehow affect his relationship. He had no reason to want to break up a marital relationship. Was it a crime, to use his desire to tend to Elvyra's spiritual side, which "lay fallow," and about which her husband had no idea?

He saw this issue completely differently when he saw Elvyra beside her unfortunate husband dedicating her entire self to him, her heart. He saw that she really did belong to someone else. In other words, what he got from her was an abundance from her generous nature, which he could appreciate like any other person. It was something that belonged to everyone and no one at the same time; it couldn't be possessed and denied or ignored! Can love exist without that feeling?

Mykolas adapted very quickly. That is, what he thought was love now seemed to be a reflection of immense gratitude toward women who understood him, who sought him out, exposed his wounds, and devoted themselves to healing them like a merciful Sister. This enriched his character and fostered dormant principles, improving his life, and also helped him reach a higher stage in his approach to life, where he clearly saw his life's purpose.

That's why, with no self-pity in the least, he now enjoyed the feelings that Julija stirred in him. He trusted himself, his best instincts, and believed that this was a path forward from his errant ways. He adored Julija's every gesture, act and word. Most of all he liked and was fascinated by her care for the children entrusted to her, the perfection with which she coped with this responsibility.

If I'd looked at women the way I look at her now, he thought, *how I would have avoided hopeless mistakes and failures!*

Taking the liberty to fantasize, Mykolas travelled very far against his will. He, a single man who was in theory a great threat to the institution of marriage, imagined himself as the head of a family, whose heart had to be Julija! If now he were to succumb to his inborn instincts, he would simply ask: "Do you want to be the mother of my children?" However, Mykolas understood right away that it would be indecent to speak this way, and besides, he believed it was much too early. That's why he remained circumspect. When they arrived into town and were near their destination, he said:

"After this I'm going to Warsaw. Do you have any problem meeting me there, at the palace? If you want to, please give me a day's notice when you're coming."

He spoke formally, giving his question no special meaning. Julija didn't how to respond or what to say.

"To tell you the truth, I don't know..." she mumbled, embarrassed. "... If you really..."

"Really!" Mykolas spoke for her, looking her in the eyes with great affection. "It depends on whether you trust your new friend, or whether you want to be rid of me..."

"I trust you, I trust you!" she assured him, with a sweet spirit.

Overjoyed, he wanted to thank her but right then the carriage stopped in front of lawyer Sushevski's house.

Mykolas was confident that he needn't be present for the reunion of the family. Besides, he saw that Julija was being helped out by servants. He heard the bell of the departing vehicle ring and ran off, lifting his hat.

"I'll just stop in the hotel for a minute," he said. "I'll book a ticket and then come to see Steponas in half an hour."

However, instead of going to the hotel, he just went off the road. He wanted to savor his thoughts. They raced ahead like a hundred spirited horses. *I've never doubted myself like that before,* he thought. *Never wanted something, sure it was right, with such a feeling of success! Where did it come from? I'm*

in such a different mood from the one I had when I arrived in Egliai.
I'm not sick and tired of life! Even if I wanted to, I wouldn't have
managed to wake such inspiration in myself that I could trust.
Today that confidence arrived from somewhere and fired me up to
the point that I couldn't see any obstacle that I couldn't get past.
Oh, sweet bliss!

Could Julija refuse me? Never! But who knows? I'm ten years
older than she is. Besides, am I worthy of this pure, innocent soul?
Do I have any right to reach a hand to the good fortune that smiles
on me?... But of course! Surely, I do. A few doubts persist, when I
compare myself now with myself earlier. If I were the same as I was,
I wouldn't have the scruples to stand before her and say: 'Be my
wife.' But now, as someone who became Elvyra's sounding board, I
surely have the right now.

It got cloudy and the area around the path looked dark.
Neither clouds nor a nasty quivering swamp could dampen
the happiness seeded in his heart. Suddenly the sun burst
through the clouds and in the blink of an eye flooded the
whole landscape.

Although he was lost in thought, Mykolas couldn't help
be surprised by the uplifting rays of sunlight. He was
astonished to notice the parallel between nature lighted up
and his own new-born feeling which like the sun bathed him
in light and happiness after his dreary life without purpose
until then.

I feel reborn, like Faust, he thought, almost running,
because he felt light as a bird and liked to move fast. *Elvyra*
did change me. Talking to her gave me insight. I learned to treasure
life and figure out the paths I need to take. Suddenly all my naïve
thoughts dispersed like those clouds, and good fortune shone on me
in the person of Julija, who, if not Elvyra, I wouldn't have
appreciated. I would have failed to seek her out and come to love her.

Still, he wondered about the bizarre fact that his love for Julija transpired so fast and with such pleasure.

That means the feeling that I just experienced and appropriately acted on in my society – that, according to Elvyra, I was carried away for the sake of society. It gives me pleasure, happiness and much hope for the future. I feel that with a life partner such as Julija, I'll always move forward, I'll become a living link in the organism of society, I'll be productive, and the family I'll create will just strengthen that link. And Elvyra?... Will she forgive the mistakes I made with her? Oh, I know she will! It's pure joy that I turned to a good path, it will make up for everything...

But I am possibly mistaken about Julija's feelings? Does she possibly belong to someone else? The thought of that gave him a bad feeling. He sighed. *No, I can't leave for Warsaw until I hear more from her. If I could just find the right time!... I have to find her!*

Having decided that, he returned to the house, where he'd just left Julija.

At about that time, Steponas, who was feeling much better that day, received the commotion and jumble in his room. The children who were held back when they first saw their ailing father gradually worked up the courage and one at a time went up to greet him, telling him the highlights of their trip, sometimes in such great detail that Elvyra, worried about the nerves of the patient, had to restrain them. Still they chattered on and on because the children's happy noise cheered up Steponas. He kidded with them, such as asking:

"And what's going on with Grandma?"

"Grandma is very sad for Daddy and sent some really good pears. She told Mr. Mykolas that the doctor will surely let Daddy eat pears," they prattled one after the other.

"Oh really! Where's Mykolas?"

"He came with us and said that your leg hurt really bad. Julija cried. He kissed Julija's hand and asked her not to be sad. He asked her over and over again…"

Steponas and Elvyra exchanged knowing looks. They diverted the conversation to another topic.

Poor Julija! She had no idea that the children would spill her private hopes and dreams. Now she sat in the living room, apart from this little family for the same reason that made Mykolas remove himself also. Julija had long ago acknowledged to herself that she was in love and that she didn't know how to deal with this feeling. She had no hopes. She kept remembering fragments from her talk with Mykolas, when he passionately said he longed for romantic, true, nurturing love, but he intended not to join his life to his beloved.

She believed that his words were honest and true, although she didn't understand the source of such a great passion – completely independent of what she felt in her heart. She didn't want to be apart from him even a minute. She wanted to become essential to him, permeate his every thought, figure in his every action, and give him everything in the world! She didn't believe that it was possible to love any other way, and any other view of Mykolas hurt her as if it were proof that he was not interested in her.

More than once she'd heard more than one man say he didn't want to marry because marriage is selfish, it limits people and keeps them away from bigger issues. At that time, she didn't listen to their opinion because it wasn't very popular. Now she wanted to refute it because she felt deeply that they were wrong. She tried to comfort herself that having just won over Mykolas' heart, all those opinions were nothing but malicious dreams. But Mykolas was leaving, and with him her hope died that they would ever meet again. His genuine expression of affection on the journey from Egliai to N. stirred a lot of hope in her. But the sudden departure put everything to an end, she thought, the sad vision of bad luck before her.

Something rustling roused her from her thoughts. Right in front of her was the one on her mind! Mykolas! Julija looked at him, quiet, and her cheeks flushed a pretty rose.

Mykolas had no idea that his fate would turn auspicious. After he rang and the maid led him into the living room, he heard the hum of children spilling out of the room in which Steponas lay. He saw that the whole bunch had gathered by the patient's bed. He noticed Julija in the living room, standing at the entrance. He saw only her profile, but her whole posture and facial expression hinted at great sadness and longing. When she saw him, she brightened with unabashed joy. Full of confidence and hope, he boldly walked over to her, put out his hand, and said:

"Miss Julija, please don't be shocked when I tell you with no introduction my heart's desire. I can't leave without knowing for sure. Will you be my wife, Miss Julija?" he asked earnestly, looking at her and squeezing the palm of her shaking hand.

She looked him in the eye. He stood in front of her, dignified and handsome. His pensive eyes expressed such love and patience, a lot of soul and kindness, that Julija replied with firm conviction:

"Yes."

He gently kissed her hand.

Involved with each other, they didn't notice that Elvyra was watching through an open door, wanting to see who'd arrived when she heard the doorbell. She was an unwilling witness to Mykolas' proposal. In her heart, she was glad but at the same time she was worried about Julija's happiness. She recalled that Mykolas had tried to use Julija to get closer to her, and it seemed ugly. Then she was ashamed to think anything like that about Mykolas at this moment.

Well then, she said to herself. *He probably already figured out that I wasn't going to fall in love with anyone but Steponas, and I hate flirting.*

She sat down next to her husband and, taking advantage of the children being busy, tried to understand the sudden change in Mykolas.

After an hour, Mykolas got ready to leave for Warsaw. There was very little time before his train departed – just enough to say good-bye to Steponas and Elvyra. Going into Steponas' room, Julija was very serious and embarrassed, where Mykolas glowed with happiness. Barely glancing at them, Elvyra guessed that Julija had accepted Mykolas' proposal, although the couple had decided to keep their engagement a secret from society for a while. As she said good-bye, she gave Mykolas her hand and joked:

"Aren't you afraid the apathy is going to come back when you return to Warsaw?"

"Oh, no! Today I can get the better of a curse like that with lots of work that waits for me there. I'm going back strong and happy." He looked at Julija and went on to Elvyra: "Thank you for everything. Believe me, I'll put my heart and soul into being a good student of yours, and deserving of happiness."

THE END

Countess Sofija and Count Vladimir Zubov –the makers of happiness for others

By Dr. Jolanta Kriuniene

Tr. from Lithuanian to English
by Dr. R. Sevo and Dr. J. Kriuniene

The novel "Laimė" [happiness] by Countess Sofija Bilevičiūtė-Zubovienė was written in Polish and published in Warsaw in 1902. It mysteriously disappeared for longer than one hundred years and could have been lost to us. The work was issued under the pseudonym of Z. Wlodowicz, which encodes the name of author and her husband: Sofija (Zofija) and Vladimir (Wlodzimierz). It's a story with autobiographical resonance, revealing the personal drama of two prominent people in the setting of a country estate in 19th Century Lithuania.

The novel was written during the period when the Zubov couple were building private schools on their estates. Sofija visited the schools and gave lessons and talks on the topic of family values. And so fiction reflects reality here: the protagonist is Elvyra, a soul sister who is Sofija's own age, "a fascinating philosopher" and the guardian of the family home. In the pages of the book Elvyra explains her concept of natural sciences[9] to the stranger Mykolas who arrives to spend the summer on the farm. She charms him and ends up in a tangle of emotions, like a reflection in the mirror of the same situation her husband Steponas found himself, with another woman. The author unravels this Gordian knot drawing on the ideals of her family values, and the story has a happy ending, but in

Sofija Bilevičiūtė

about ten years [after the novel was written], real life turned out differently…

Recognizing himself in the story, the author's husband Vladimir Zubov bought up and destroyed the whole print run. The only copies remaining where those the author gave away to someone. The translation published here uses a copy found in the library of Sofija Bilevičiūtė's great-grandchild Dalia Palukaitienė. From its pages, we can easily figure out what motivated a lady of the manor to write a novel like this. However, the novel isn't the only witness to the circumstances of its writing. The story can also be explained by the twists and turns of the author's biography.

---

[9] Sofija Bilevičiūtė-Zubovienė explained her concept more fully later in a scientific treatise: "The benefit of an awareness of the laws of nature, which we instinctively obey."

The Bilevičiai (Billewicz, Bielewicz, Bilewicz) are an old noble family, members of the elite of Žemaitija province. According to legends passed down, an associate of the Great King Gediminas called Žadeika had two sons: Norvilas and Bilius. The Bilevičiai (Biliūnai) family descended from the

Ipolitas Bilevičius

latter. Another more unlikely legend claims that the royal Žadeika of Žemaitija received as a gift the sister of the Great King Vytautas, called Milušą (Miklausę), to be his wife. They had two sons: Biliaus and Mąstvilas. This version of the legend mixes fiction (e.g., the marriage to Vytautas' sister) and true facts (e.g., actual historical people Bilius and Mąstvilas).[10]

---

[10] E. Saviščevas, Bilevičių kilmė ir genealogija (XV–XVI a.) // *Lituanistica*, T. 4(48), 2001, p. 4.

Elena Daugirdaitė-Bilevičienė with her daughters: Joana Narutavičienė (below), Sofija Zubovienė (standing), Elena Viercinskienė, Stanislava Zaikauskienė, about 1880

According to Konstantinas Jablonskis' data,[11] the Biliūnai arrived to Žemaitija from a locale near Vilnius (near

---

[11] K. Jablonskis, Mažvydo gyvenimas is aplinka // K. Jablonskis. *Lietuvių kultūra ir jos veikėjai*, Vilnius, 1973, p. 23–24.

Maišiagala) at the beginning of the 16th Century. The seat of their residence was the Biliūnas estate near Raseiniai. Structures of the estate built around 1427 survive to this day and have been restored. Juozas Girdzijauskas identifies an elder Jonas Biliūnas-Bilevičius within one of the first cultural communities concentrated around Žemaitija in the middle of the 16th Century.[12] The latter was a rural overseer in Beržėnai and Didžiujų Dirvėnai – as such an Administrator for the Great King. After the death of his cousin Jurgis Biliūnas, together with Jonas Kmita he became the leader over all the lands of Žemaitija. Jonas Biliūnas befriended the Magistrate of the last Crusader's Order Albrechtas Brandenburgiečis, and was supported and promoted by him, as they zealously spread the Reformation in Žemaitija. On his own estate Viduklė he gathered people who turned out to be pioneers of the written Lithuanian language in Lithuanian history, as they helped envision a national culture. There were also Abraomas Kulvietis, Stanislovas Rapolionis, Martynas Mažvydas, Jurigs Zablockis, Aleksandras Rodūnionis Vyresnysis and others.

Research by Mykolas Biržiška found the following in later pages of the family history: "In the 18th–19th Century some called themselves Bilevičiai, while others – Biliūnai, or split off to Stankevičiai. In the 16th–18th Century they were Rietavas, Dirvėnai, Beržėnai, Ariogala, Šeduva and other patriarchs, Stalininkai (Dapifer) and Pastalininkai, elders, officials and others. In the 17th-19th Centuries in Raseiniai, Šiauliai, they were judges in the royal court and officials. Very often the Bilevičiai family were related to Ginetos-

---

[12] Juozas Girdzijauskas, Žemaičių kulturiniai sambūriai XVI–XIX a. // *Viduklė*, Kaunas: Naujasis Lankas, 2002, p. 154–167.

Pilsudskiai."[13] (By the way, Sofija Bilevičiūtė-Zubovienė was a second cousin of the Polish General Juzef Pilsudski.) The Bilevičiai family was commemorated by the prominent Polish writer, Nobel Laureate Henrikas Sienkevičius in his own novel "Tvanas" [Deluge].

Sofija Bilevičiūtės' father Ipolitas Bilevičius (1822–1901) managed the Aušbikavis estate near Raseiniai. He was a writer who studied philosophy in his free time, and in 1902 issued his book in Polish "Thoughts About God" with the subtitle "Or about the human condition." It is no coincidence that the same philosophical themes are characteristic of his daughter's novel "Laimė." In addition, Bilevičius translated Jean de La Fontaine's fables into Polish, and works by Adomas Mickevičius into French. He worked in Žemės Bank in Vilnius. He married Elena Daugirdaitę from the Klišiai estate near Viekšniai – according to genealogy, she was a distant relative through one of Bilius' sons, Daugirdas, mentioned in a 15th Century source, who founded the Daugirdai family.

Sofija Bilevičiūtė-Zubovienė and the historian and writer Balys Sruogas' wife Vanda Daugirdaitė-Sruogienė were descended from a common great grandfather Antanas Daugirdas (1783–1856). Her parents Ipolitas and Elena Bilevičiai had five sons: Konradas, Pranciškus, Adomas, Steponas, Zigmantas, and four daughters: Elena, Sofija, Joana and Stanislava. One of the sisters, Joana, later married the landowner Stanislovas Narutavičius, a signer of the

---

[13] Mykolas Biržiška, *Iš mūsų kulturos ir literatūros istorijos*. Kaunas, 1938, p. 84.

Independence Act on February 16, 1918, and a brother of the first President of Poland, Gabrielius Narutavičius.

Sofija was born in Kaunas in 1860 and spent her childhood at home on the Aušbikavis estate. Here's what Pranas Budkus, who was born on that estate, remembers: "The Aušbikavis estate was surrounded by trees on all sides. They didn't practice anything foreign to locals. Here the old Lithuanian traditions were well preserved. People in Aušbikavis still spoke in the core (central) Žemaitija dialect. ... The mansion on the Aušbikavis estate was called 'numas' [not 'namas']. Numas was all boards,[14] and the roof was shingles. There were two chimneys, big windows – four stories.[15] Farmhouses on that estate were called 'budinkais.' ... When the people of Aušbikavis still lived in tents, then there was no Aušbikavis estate yet. Actually, according to Count Mantrimas, the Polish King granted the Aušbikavis grounds to Count Bilevičius along with the grounds belonging to Count Mantrimas. Because of that, Count Mantrimas was forced to travel to Warsaw to prove to King Zigmantas Augustas his legal and royal right to his own property. According to Mantrimas, if he hadn't been able to accomplish that, he would have been forced to be a serf to the Bilevičiai."[16]

In 1872 Sofija moved to Vilnius with her parents and finished her middle schooling at the Emilija Vrublevska Polish school, and after that, entered in the next to last class of the Russian state gymnasium. She travelled abroad a great

---

[14] Sheathed with boards on the sides
[15] There were frames called "remai" to hold the glass in the windows. (LKŽ).
[16] Mano senolių gimtinė. Prano Budkaus atsiminimų fragmentai // Žemaičių žemė, 2008, No. 2, p. 59.

deal with her father. In 1880 she enrolled in the famous Bestužev course in Petersburg – the only higher education in imperial Russia available to women. She studied natural sciences and pedagogy. She was the first of Lithuanian's woman to enroll in higher education. She met Vladimir Zubov in Petersburg. He was studying natural sciences at the university. Their friendship and social relationship began through group activities. They married on August 6, 1884 and after finishing their studies, settled in Šiauliai, then later in Ginkūnai, where they built a new house following Sofija Zubovienė's own design (clearly, only the layout of rooms).

The Bilevičiai noble family of Žemaitija (about 1885). From left to right: standing Konradas Bilevičius, Sofija Bilevičiutė-Zubovienė, her husband Vladimiras Zubovas, Stanislava Bilevičiutė-Zaikauskienė; seated Pranciškus Bilevičius, Adomas Bilevičius, between them Zigmantas Bilevičius, Elena Daugirdaitė-Bilevičienė, Ipolitas Bilevičius; standing Steponas Bilevičius, seated Joana Bilevičiutė-Narutavičienė, holding a photograph of Elena Bilevičiūtė-Viercinskienė and J. Viercinskis.

Vladimir Zubov (1862–1933) was raised in the famous Zubov dynasty, whose roots reach back to the second half of the 13th Century, under the rule of the Mongol-Tartars in Russia. The oldest ancestor in the family, Abraham, was an Administer for the Golden Horde Khan. He was christened with the name Zacharija. His heirs were Russian, who took as wives Italians, Spaniards, and Tatars. One of his descendants had the last name Zub, which was the root of the Zubov name.[17]

Probably the most prominent personality in the family, Platon Zubov – a favorite of Catherine II, statesman, general-in-chief, and Duke – was granted the fruits of the Šiauliai economy by Empress Catherine II in 1793 as a meritorious reward for expanding the Empire. Suspended from his governing duties, Platon resided in Joniškis, and later in Rundalė. He lived in luxury and bought and sold many farms. He purchased Ginkūnai in 1805.

After his death in 1822, Dimitri inherited his farms in Lithuania – the only one of four brothers who was not involved the conspiracy to murder Paul I and who was not interested in palace intrigues. Dimitri Zubov (1764–1836) settled in Šiauliai and became the founder of the branch of Lithuanian Zubovs. For a period, Dimitri managed Ginkūnai as the economic center of the estate.[18] His son Nikolajus (1801–1871) build the manors in Šiauliai. He married Countess Aleksandrą de Raymond de Mormoiron (1807–1839) of Italian-French descent, and had four children: Nikolajus and Gabrielius, Elžbietą and Aleksandrą.

---

[17] V. Veteikis, *Ąžuolas plačiašakis*. Šiauliai, 1995, p. 1.
[18] V. Jokšas, Zubovai: istoriniai portretai // *Komjaunimo tiesa*, 1989 12 07, p. 4.

Nikolajus Nikolajevičius Zubov (1832–1898), the father of the husband of this book's author, mostly lived in Šiauliai, in Didžiadvaris. He was a gentle man at home, loved his grandchildren, and highly respected their mother, his daughter-in-law, Sofija Bilevičiūtė-Zubovienė. He was famous as a public figure: he was the noble leader of the Šiauliai region, and after 1878 the noble leader of the Kaunas province also.

Under his administration economic development and industry progressed a great deal. Nikolajus Zubov was the initiator and sponsor of agricultural exhibitions held in Šiauliai – the gatherings that started in 1875. The first event was written up in the Polish newspaper "Tygodnik Ilustrowany" [Weekly Illustrated]. There the Count featured production of bricks and woolen fabric. In the province (the suburbs of Šiauliai) Nikolajus built a large flour mill, a plant for processing coarse metal into agricultural tools, and around 1867 a modern beer brewery. Before the First World War, the brewery produced about 300,000 buckets of beer in a year, worth about 3,600,000 Litas. The brewery declined during the war and just began to recover in 1922, when a limited liability established itself under Volf-Engelman. The Zubovs traded all the dwellings with 40 hectares of land for shares. Processing in the recovered brewery reached 500,000 liters the first year. The brewery before the war and after was led by an experienced director – the engineer Bielskis. It was said that due to the management of the company, the quality of the beer deteriorated and consumption declined.[19]

In 1890, under Nikolajus, a project was started to build telephone poles to connect the provincial capital and the

---

[19] Akc. alaus bravoras b-vė "Gubernija" // *Diena*, 1931 03 29, p. 10.

Ginkūnai estate. In 1902 a small electrical power plant was opened in the Province: in the evenings, when the city center of Šiauliai was dark, the Provincial streets were lit with incandescent lamps. There were several other large industries in Aleksandria: a brickyard, and a glazed Dutch tile factory. It's clear that bricks manufactured in the brickyard in Aleksandria were used to build the Didžiadvaris gymnasium [higher school] and the St. George church. Not one of these factories is operating any more.

Nikolajus and his wife Aleksandra Olsufjevaitė-Zubovienė (1840–1913) supported cultural-artistic, charity, and educational organizations. One of the first – "Žiburėlis" [Light], established in 1894 by Gabrielė Petkevičaitė and Jadvyga Juškytė, had a chapter in Šiauliai. The organization made it possible for many capable children from poor families to attend school. It sponsored [notable people] Žemaitė, Julius Janonis, Vincas Kudirka, Kipras Petrauskas, and others. In 1875 Countess Aleksandra opened in Šiauliai a shelter for seniors and a shelter for children and the disabled, that were sustained until the First World War.

In addition, she established and sponsored a hostel for girls in Šiauliai which in 1898 was reorganized into a gymnasium [higher school] for girls (now Didžiadvaris Gymnasium). After 1869 the Zubovs allocated annual funding of 1200 rubles, and in 1898 they provided a plot of land and the construction of a brick building. In the Šiauliai facility, girls studied for four years, while in Kaunas or Vilnius provinces, they studied only two and three years. Teacher training for residential teachers was begun for the first time in the Šiauliai school.

After 1876, students at the regular provincial gymnasium in Šiauliai were given a stipend in the name of

Nikolajus Zubov. In 1910, the Countess established in Bubiai a three-year program in animal husbandry and dairy farming, and she directed and sustained an orphanage.

In 1895 Aleksandra Olsufjevaitė-Zubovienė wrote to Tsar Alexander III and made the case that it was immoral to force students who were not Orthodox to pray for the Tsar in the Orthodox church. The Tsar offered to read the letter and annotated a resolution: "If it's true that this harms our young people, it's worth thinking about it." In the summer of 1897 he ordered that Catholic students not be forced to pray in the Orthodox Church.

In 1874, a group of left-leaning gymnasium students led by Jonas Bielskis secretly organized an illegal literature library. Aleksandra donated books, and when the library was in danger, took it into her residence. Books from the flat of one pupil were put into a child's wagon, leashed to a small pony, and transported by her own children Olga and Dimitri. It didn't occur to anyone that the children were engaged in an activity against the government. Once the books were in a secure library, they were delivered to readers by the oldest Zubov child Vladimir, himself a student. There were about 3000 volumes of books in the library. In 1883, the publisher Miglovara (J. Miliauskas), who knew the overseer of the library Jonas Beržanskis, an eighth grader in the gymnasium, sent over issues of "Aušra" [Dawn], which Jonas distributed through the Šiauliai market – and that way the newspaper reached farmers' houses.[20]

Aleksandra, the first Zubov to concern herself with the culture of the local people, sensed a nationalist movement.

---

[20] Juozas Normantas, Gedimino palikuonys Žemaitijoje // Žemaičių žemė, 2001, Nr. 1, p. 42.

Jonas Fledžinskas who worked on the Ginkūnai estate wrote about her in his memoir: "She was an extraordinary older lady: petite, thin, lively, with a gracious and sweet manner. If you ignored her high status [...] and the fact that she'd spent her early years among the highest classes (a lady-in-waiting in the Tsar's palace), she was entirely unpretentious, accepting everyone and warm and gracious to everyone. She supported a lot of young people, to whom she regularly distributed allowances from her trust funds."[21] The Countess Aleksandra died on September 14, 1913, during a visit to Nikolsko-Viazemski in the Tula province. She wasn't buried according to the usual Zubov tradition in the family cemetery at St. Valerijonas near Petersburg, where the last Zubov buried was her husband Nikolajus Zubov, but rather according to her wishes, in Lithuania, in an Orthodox cemetery near the Beinoriškės farm in an old section of Bubiai.

Nikolajus and Aleksandra Zubov had four children: Vladimir, Marija, Olga and Dimitri. Vladimir Zubov, the husband of this book's author, was born on March 18, 1862, in Šiauliai. His mother did not keep him from mixing with peasant children. He learned Lithuanian and Polish languages.[22] When the boy turned nine years old, his father hired the most reputable teacher at that time, Laurynas Ivinskis, to prepare him for entrance to the gymnasium. Here is how Count Vladimir remembered his teacher, looking back:

---

[21] Jonas Fledžinskas, *Atsiminimai*, Šiauliai, 1997, p. 36.
[22] Vladimiras Zubovas, Zubovai ir Zubovienės Lietuvoje // *Santara*, 1992 vasara, p. 90.

"Ivinskis – a very nice old man... You have no idea how he loved me. And I loved and respected him deeply. I called him 'Uncle.' ... He was a learned man, a scientist, specializing in botany. When my father learned of this very nice old man, he invited him and gave him housing and a living allowance, looking after all his creature comforts to make it possible for him to quietly and seriously do the work of teaching and the work of the homeland.

"While he lived with us at Didžiadvaris in Šiauliai, he was on the first floor of a house that's a hostel now. His friend and colleague A. Moro had already been living upstairs for a long time. Two rooms were assigned to him.

"I spent many days visiting him in those rooms. He would read to me and lecture, and I would listen. [...] I won't lie when I tell you that in Ivinskis' room, enfolded in this uncle's heart, was the very first time I began to love our homeland and began to speak Lithuanian. He had my word, before he left for Plungę, that when I finish gymnasium studies in Šiauliai, I'll go into science, and when I finish my advanced studies, I'll come back home and work in Lithuania. It wasn't hard to give him my word and fulfill my uncle's wishes...

"He gave me his guide to Lithuanian plants (herbarium) and a wonderful album of Lithuanian mushrooms (with illustrations in Ivinskis' perfect hand!). When I finished university in Petersburg and left for home, I donated these to the Petersburg science department for general studies, from which I graduated."[23]

---

[23] Juozas Tumas, *Lietuvių literatūros paskaitos:* draudžiamasis laikas, Laurynas Ivinskis, kovotojai. Kaunas, 1924, p. 22.

Three Vladimir Zubovs in front of the
Šiauliai higher school, commemorating
its 75th anniversary, in 1926.

Ivinskis lived on the Zubov's estate and taught young
Vladimir from the autumn of 1871 through the summer of
1874. In addition to Ivinskis, the children were prepared for
gymnasium by Jonas Bielskis (1855–1904), a participant in the
revolutionary movement, who around 1874 organized the

aforementioned library of progressive literature in the Šiauliai gymnasium. He had a significant influence on Zubov's thinking. During the same autumn at the end of 1874, Vladimir entered the third class in Šiauliai gymnasium. The Zubovs were letting their oldest son continue his studies in the gymnasium, and not in the Cadet Corps which was traditional for nobility. Already at this time he was known for espousing a socialist ideology. It is interesting that three Zubov generations graduated from the same gymnasium, all of them named Vladimir – grandfather, father and son.

Having finished the Šiauliai gymnasium, during 1881–1886 Vladimir Zubov studied natural science at Petersburg University, specifically chemistry with Dmitri Mendelejev. As mentioned before, in Petersburg he met the woman who would become his wife, Sofija Bilevičiūtė. He continued advanced study in Halle, Germany, which he finished in the Veterinary Academy.

In 1882 Jonas Šliūpas arrived in Petersburg to study natural science and became active in forming what was probably the first Lithuanian student's patriotic association. This was when the ownership of serfs was abolished [in Imperial Russia]. Soon Lithuanian students came to see him. "They were divided into two groups: one around J. Kymantas (a lawyer), who followed the direction of P. Vileišis; the other revolved around the man from Šiauliai, Vl. Zubov, in whose rooms about 50 people gathered, mostly leaning toward socialism. Šliūpas was involved in both groups; he wanted to coordinate them. The nationalists studied Lithuanian language, history, and literature, where the socialists worked in the field of economics."[24]

While a student in Petersburg, Vladimir Zubov engaged in activities of the Lithuanian-Polish socialist party "Proletariat," and he was a member of the Central Committee [Centro Komitetas]. Sofija Bilevičiūtė, like her husband, had a close relationship with young people in "Proletariat." Nikolajus Zubov was not happy with his son's revolutionary activities, but he tolerated them.[25]

In his memoirs Šliūpas was witness to that time:

"When I moved to Petersburg in the autumn of 1882, I joined the Lithuanian group [...]. I got to know Vl. Zubov, Meyro and a few other Lithuanian estate-holders, who were also huddled in their own cluster, a group that kept itself separate from the Lithuanian fellowship. But I eased them up and we came together [...] in Zubov's rooms. [...] When I was run out of Petersburg, I lost track of what was going on with the Petersburg people.

"In the summer of 1883 I taught at the Zubov home. There I was able to meet more often with the noble revolutionaries. I wrote a little pamphlet: 'The Problem, its roots, dimensions, and solutions.' I also wrote two other very hot-headed brochures.

"Not far from Kuršėnai, at the Bilevičiai estate, there was a gathering in mid-summer of all the younger nobility of Žemaitija. There we discussed political-economic solutions for the country, and wrote up a mandate for the revolution.

---

[24] P. Jonėkas, Lietuvybės būreliai tautinio atgimino priešaušry // *Trimitas*, 1940, Nr. 25, p. 615.
[25] Vladimiras Zubovas, Zubovai ir Zubovienės Lietuvoje // *Santara*, 1992 vasara, p. 88.

Copies probably reached the Bilevičius father, who found out about the concerns of the young people this way. A rumor was spread among the Žemaitija nobility that we were 'bad revolutionaries.' That if Zubov or Janavičiaus hadn't been with us, the nobility would have turned us commoners over to the authorities. This time they just threatened us."[26]

After his father's death, deeply influenced by socialist ideals and his own teachers Liudvikas Janavičiaus and Jonas Bielskis, Vladimir even wanted to give up his inherited properties and title, and join the underground. But Bielskis himself talked him out of it – telling him that he would be more useful to the socialist movement if he kept his property and authority.

In 1888 there was a gathering of the "Proletariat" in Zurich. Vladimir Zubov, apparently persuaded by his wife, formally left the party. Nevertheless, he continued to support the movement, issuing left-leaning newsletters, financing revolutionaries, and recruiting them to his estate and his schools. He rescued the social-democratic leader Vincas Mickevičius-Kapsukas – in 1914 he hid him on his estate in Medemrodė after he escaped from Siberia. There Kapsukas was burrowed with his sister-in-law Aldona Didžiulytė (Kazanavičienė), who taught children of the estate workers. Later on, Zubov helped him flee to Tilžė. He also financed other political entities fighting against Tsarism, especially a national group called Varpininkai.[27] Later he became closer to the Lithuanian people's socialists.

---

[26] Iš dr. J. Šliupo atsiminimų // *Nepriklausomoji Lietuva*, 1919 08 20, p. 1.
[27] Lithuanian activists associated with the newspaper „Varpas" [The Bell].

Almost every year in the Šiauliai environs around the Zubov estate there was a pretend folk festival that was really a gathering to organize for the independence of Lithuania. The first event was in June 12 of 1899, at Aleksandra's manor. Intelligentsia, socialist and nationalist revivalists gathered from all over Lithuania. While some danced and partied, "honestly" treated and made Russian officials drunk, others secretly worked on the task of forming a nation. Seeing the Lithuanian intelligentsia gathering, the Russians sensed the purpose of the festival, but Count Zubov, Orthodox and authoritative in the eyes of the Russian officials, hid and shielded a lot.

Between the two wars there was a barn still standing on Aleksandra's estate, and the first festival was held in front of it. A stone was built in the brick wall of that barn to commemorate the first gathering. Now the barn is gone. At the festival in Dabikinė in 1903, the Varpininkai Lithuanian national organization led by Povilas Višinskis founded the first Lithuanian democratic party, which in an independent Lithuania was renamed Peoples Populist Party and was the second political force for statehood after the Christian Democrats. The largest gathering of Lithuanian intellectuals was called in June of 1904, at Kairiai. There were about 300 participants, and among them, Jonas Jablonskis, Juozas Ambrozaitis, Vladas Putvinskis, Marija Pečkauskaitė, Juozas Tumas-Vaižgantas, Povilas Višinskis. While the performances were held in the estate's barn, in the mansion were people discussing how to fight the Tsar's government.

The Russian government deferred to Count Zubov although they didn't like him: this was widely known, at that time, about the Governor General in Vilnius who would tour Šiauliai. The local "little king" over Šiauliai and the surroundings, a "police officer," decided to meet the honored guest coming from Vilnius properly and asked Vladimir Zubov to lend him a carriage to transport him. He invited the Count to meet him at the rail station himself. The Count agreed. Soon the "Supreme Excellency" proudly stepped from the first-class car at the rail station. He walked among the local leaders, approached Count Zubov and held out his hand, saying: "Ah, it's you, Count. I advise you to have more Russian soul." Count Zubov had a memorable response to this remark. Without a word, he put his hand in his pocket, got into the carriage that was ready for the Governor, and drove off alone to his Ginkūnai estate.[28]

Vladimir Zubov (the first)

---

[28] Viktoras Biržiška, Lietuvių teisių gynėjas T. Vrublevskis // *Trimitas*, 1935, Nr. 15, p. 268.

In the transition period between the 19th and 20th Centuries, in large part thanks to Vladimir Zubov, Šiauliai became one of the most important centers of Lithuanian nationalism, where famous leaders were active in the movement, such as Augustinas Janulaitis, Julija and Veronika Janulaitytės, Marija Pečkauskaitė, Povilas Višinskis, Gabrielė Petkevičaitė-Bitė. When he lived in Petersburg, Zubov started the "Grūdo" [Grain] group to help war refugees. He was one of the founders of the newspaper "Naujoji Lietuva" [New Lithuania] and a member of the editorial board. He himself wrote articles on social and cultural issues. He wrote political pieces under the pseudonym "Dantis". [Tooth; because the root of his name "Zub" means "tooth" in Russian]

Sofija and Vladimir Zubov accomplished a lot in the field of education too – they built Lithuanian schools for the children of workers on their estates and from the villages nearby. In 1890 the couple settled in Ginkūnai. Starting in 1896 they opened the doors of the mansion's basement to the first secret school. (In 1933 it was named for Sofija and Vladimir Zubov). The two nobles had structures built especially for schools, supported them, provided supplies, provided textbooks to students free of charge, and paid the teachers' salaries. The teachers in Zubov schools received twice the salary as those working in government schools. The schools were spacious and comfortable, and they always emphasized being an example for neatness and cleanliness. "Little went on without observing the high standards of Count Zubov. There aren't many like him among Suduva landowners. It's a shame we don't have more people like the Zubovs," was written in the press.[29]

---

[29] Žinios // Lietuvos žinios, 1911 01 13, p. 3.

The government school inspector for the Kaunas province, A. Itomlenskis, remembers when he paid a visit to the Zubov schools, they were of such high quality that the initial school director P. Kukuškinas once asked the Count to let him propose to the Tsar that he grant an Order of Excellence, but Zubov disdained the idea: "I don't work for the blessings of the Tsar."[30]

Sofija Bilevičiūtė-Zubovienė with her husband and children, 1872.

---

[30] A. Itomlenskis, Atsiminimai apie V. Zubová ir Sofija Zubovienę // *Naujoji Romuva*, 1936, Nr. 44, p. 871.

The schools established by the Zubovs in Ginkūnai, Naisiai, Gubernija, Dabikinė and Medemrodė were official, teaching in the Russian language, but secretly they also taught in the Lithuanian language. After 1905, after the ban on the press was repealed, the schools were officially taught in Lithuanian. Some Russian teachers left on their own, and progressive Lithuanians worked in the schools, for the most part women: J. Juškytė, three sisters Landsbergaitės (daughters of Gabrieliaus Žemkalnis); later J. Petrauskaitė (Nainienė), L. Tomkytė.

Sofija Zubovienė inspected the schools herself and improved the educational curriculum. (In the third grade, Lithuanian history was required to be taught, along with geography. She directed that more attention be devoted to arithmetic and that it be taught in Lithuanian.) She taught natural science herself and gave tutorials to poor students, as well as clothes, and even food. (Every year she allocated about 10,000 rubles from her own funds). At Christmas time a tree was decorated with toys and gifts. Depending on the audience, the Countess read stories to the parents of students in Lithuanian, Russian and Polish – about family values, how to behave nicely, the subject of running a house and a farm, how to write petitions, business writing. She promoted Darwin's theory of evolution, which frightened the rural women. They said, "Lady, you probably don't believe in God..." She loved to talk to young people personally, telling them about her experience in life.

Sofija and her husband wanted to set up a teacher's seminary in Šiauliai, which would prepare new teachers for the schools. For this mission, they allocated a plot of land two hectares[31] in size in the Šiauliai city center and provided funding. While it was being built, they housed the seminary on the premises of their mansion in Didžiadvaris. The teachers' seminary was planned to open in the fall of 1914, however, the First World War started and the project was interrupted. After the War in 1922, the Zubovs donated the parkland around the Didžiadvaris mansion to the city of Šiauliai. There was a notice in the press in 1928 that the Education Ministry bought two buildings in Šiauliai for 137 thousand Litas from "a representative of Zubovienė, which will host a teachers' seminary and a model early school."[32] The seminary was in operation through 1957, and after that was reorganized as the Pedagogic Institute. Now it is a part of Šiauliai University, housing the art faculty.

During the years when the Lithuanian press was banned, the Zubovs distributed secret Lithuanian publications. Didžiadvaris was one of the distribution points where the contraband publication was brought. It was brought there from storage in Gubernija, and, to avoid detection, spread to surrounding farms and towns in barrels from the beer brewery.[33] Later it was transported as "Varpas" [The Bell], "Ūkininkas" [Farmer], "Darbininkų balsas" [Worker's Voice], even "Iskra" [Furrow] and other social-democratic publications.

---

[31] 1 Hectare = 2.47105381 Acres. Hectare is a metric system area unit and widely used globally for land measurement, agriculture and forestry. It equals to 10,000 square meters. The abbreviation is "ha".

[32] Kronika // *Lietuva*, 1928 01 19, p. 6; Lietuvos naujienos // *Šiaulių naujienos*, 1928 01 29, p. 1.

[33] Vladas Putvinskis, Kai lietuvišką spauda draudė // *Trimitas*, 1929 05 16, p. 328.

In 1900, Šiauliai's public library open reading room settled into the second story of the Didžiadvaris manor. Here Zubov donated an economics archive and his whole personal library to Šiauliai which included publications from 1832 from the closed Vilnius University. The first librarian arrived in Šiauliai in 1903 – the linguist Jonas Jablonskis, who organized the Šiauliai economics archives. The Šiauliai public library was open to all interested readers, and for this reason it is considered the origin of the city's public library.

At the beginning of the First World War, the Šiauliai public library was transported to Russia, and reached Rostov near the Donau, where it was looted by local people. What remained of the Šiauliai economics archive was partly destroyed by the German occupying forces. Practically nothing remained after that. As Biržiška said, "We lost the richest Šiauliai economics archive with irreplaceable material describing Lithuania's economic stages, along with most of the economics collection, and decrees about witches, and 18th Century material that would shed light on the peasants' political Reform Movement, and 18th Century writings and documents in Lithuanian, and so on."[34]

After the repeal of the ban on the Lithuanian press, Šiauliai social leaders – Povilas Višinskis, Vladimir Zubov, Jonas Jablonskis and others considered how to start a newspaper. They formed an official board to issue a newspaper funded by Zubov, submitted a name for the newspaper and an editor (Višinskis), but it was not meant to be: the permit was denied.

Aside from politics and education, Vladimir Zubov was involved in agricultural business – he has a role in history as

---

[34] Vaclova Biržiška, *Knygotyros darbai*. Vilnius, 1998, p. 67, 206–207.

an innovator in animal husbandry and as an exemplary farmer who modernized the farms at Ginkūnai and his other estates (Medemrodė, Dabikinė). Overall the land and forests under his authority was up to 4000 hectares [nearly 10,000 acres]. Since he was a veterinarian and animal husbandry expert, he handled the most important decisions on the farm himself: he imported farming machines from Germany; from Denmark, breeding cattle; carried out research in order to increase the productivity of the cattle; and markedly improved the Lithuanian brown-breed of cows.

In Ginkūnai he installed a shallow cattle-shed from which manure was removed every day. He was the first to do milk production control. In 1896, the first dairy factory was developed in Ginkūnai. In its brand shop in Šiauliai, on the premises of pharmacies at the time (the corner of Varpo–Aušros street) fresh milk could be purchased with the label on the bottle: "Ginkūnai – Zubov." Later when he lived in Medemrodė, he produced the best butter in Lithuania, labelled with a little red calf.

Between the Wars there was even a scandal about an irregular "trademark:" the Count's dairy had sold the right to market its brand of butter to only one milk outlet in Kaunas. However, his trademarked butter label appeared in many stores, but on regular butter. After he learned about it, Zubov charged about 100 Kaunas milk distributors with legal liability, for using his butter label illegally.[35]

---

[35] 100 pieninių teisman // *Diena*, 1933 05 28, p. 1.

Aleksandra and Vladimir, children of Vladimir and Sofija Zubov with their governess in Ginkūnai, 1900.

In addition, he bred horses, and improved sheep and pig varieties. At Šiauliai's fifth agricultural exposition, Zubov's pigs got gold and silver medals.[36] He did not neglect vegetables: he reclaimed meadows and soils, experimented with high-yield seeds to increase production and to adapt to the conditions of particular soil.

Before the First World War, on his estates, Zubov banned work "from sundown to sunrise" and introduced 10-hour working days during the summer months, raised the workers' wages, and concerned himself not only with the material welfare of his workers, but also their health – services of the estate's health caretaker were free of charge. Veterinary services were provided to the surrounding area by the gentleman himself.

---

[36] Šiaulių paroda // *Lietuva*, 1926 08 25, p. 4.

The Count sold bricks to people nearby for a favorable price, to encourage more beautiful buildings around the farm. He promoted innovation not only in his own territory: he participated in agricultural expositions in Šiauliai and in Vilnius, taught local farmers, opened a dairy course in Ginkūnai, and liked to invite visiting farmers to his own estate. A credit union was started in Šiauliai to support business operations, Land farmers-workers-shareholders "Progresas" [Progress] association. He was a successful farmer in Lithuania between the Wars – during that time, the Medemrodė estate under his management had an exemplary farm.

Sofija and Vladimir Zubov had two children – a son Vladimir (1887–1959) and daughter Aleksandra (1891–1961). Vladimir, like his father, befriended the children of workers from childhood on. He learned to speak Lithuanian with a Šiauliai dialect. He was taught Russian by a nanny brought from Petersburg. Within the family, he spoke Polish, and with his father's relatives Russian.

There were many guests at Ginkūnai all the time: many of them intimates of Sofija Bilevičiūtė-Zubovienė, or families of her husband's brother Dimitrijus from Bubiai, or sister Olga from the Pamūšis estate. Sometimes the host's sister Marija arrived, engaged to Sergei, the son of the great Russian writer Leo Tolstoy. Nearly every summer, Sofija and Vladimir and their children stayed at *Yasnaya Polyana* with the Tolstoys. Their daughter Aleksandra remembers sitting on Tolstoy's knee, when he taught her to eat a cucumber by scooping it out with small spoon.[37]

---

[37] Jonas Fledžinskas, *Atsiminimai*, Šiauliai, 1997, p. 40.

Count Sergei Tolstoy played the piano perfectly – beautiful concerts were performed at Ginkūnai when he visited. The Ginkūnai family was also very musical: Sofija Bilevičiūtė-Zubovienė and her daughter played piano, Vladimir Zubov played violin, and his son, the cello. According to his son-in-law Fledžinskas, "The father didn't have great technique, but his music was very expressive and emotional."[38]

Other activities enjoyed by those on the estate: the young people played croquet and tennis in the summer, while the older ones played cards. The Zubovs were hospitable not only to their relatives – in Professor Steponas Kairis' words, "the doors to their home were always open to the outside world." The latter had this impression from his visit to Ginkūnai: "There was nothing like it, the way they lived. In the entryway to a spacious wooden residence there was no a livery-clothed servant, you had to open the door yourself. Inside, if they were home, the host himself would greet you, stocky, a fine figure, round and always with a pleasant smile on his face and very often without a word offering the visitor his nicely shaven, full cheek for a kiss. There were always talks, speeches full of passion, sometimes a biting joke. Sofija Zubovienė-Bilevičiūtė [...] was quite reserved. You could explain her reserve any way you want – it was her characteristic or key to not forgetting her social standing..."[39] "The father was good-humored and mischievous – he liked to play jokes,"[40] seconded Jonas Fledžinskas.

---

[38] Ten pat, p. 60.
[39] Steponas Kairys, *Lietuva budo*, Čikaga, 1957, p. 157.
[40] Jonas Fledžinskas, *Atsiminimai*, Šiauliai, 1997, p. 16.

The Count's acrimony was quite distinct. Demonstrating his democratic outlook, he often shocked the nobility with crude jokes and cynical statements: once he treated a lady and offered her a box of candy with live frogs; once he frightened a teacher by dressing his son like a bear. The Dukes Vasilčikovai of Jurbarkas didn't invite the Count to their party ("Listen, you can't give that man a place at our table!").[41] That's why in the memories of people in his employ and farmhands he was a good, unpretentious person...

Vladimir Zubov's son Vladimir got his first lessons from his mother, Sofija Bilevičiūtė-Zubovienė. She was a teacher herself, and it seems she didn't want to trust others to shape the foundation for her son's character. Later on, there were trained teachers and governesses to develop the children. Their first teacher Tatjana Molas later married the host's brother Dimitrijus. Actually, three foreign language teachers were in residence on the estate – at first the children learned French, then German and finally English.

The son Vladimir, like his father, finished Šiauliai gymnasium and studied at Halle University (in Germany) – in agricultural studies, finishing a dissertation and earning a doctorate in 1910. While still a student he married the teacher Ona Jakubauskaitė. In Halle, his son the "third" Vladimir Zubov (1909–2007) was born. That Vladimir became the husband of M. K. Čiurlionis' daughter Danutė.

The second Vladimir, called "Papunis" among the family, for the most part continued the work of his father. Living on the Dabikinė estate after 1910, he conducted scientific research to increase the productivity of the Black

---

[41] Vladimiras Zubovas, Zubovai ir Zubovienės Lietuvoje // *Santara*, 1992 vasara, p. 92.

and White cattle. He was an experienced horseman, participating in agricultural expositions. Between the Wars he sold Dabikinė and lived in Naujadvaris, later Judreliai, which was nationalized when the Russians occupied Lithuania.

Vladimir Zubov and his son

When he resigned from the ongoing cattle research group dear to Vladimir [the father] after the Second World War, he worked in the Lithuania Department of Agriculture, at the Lithuanian Veterinary Academy, LMA Biological Institute departments, carried out studies for the botanical gardens in Dotnuva and Kaunas, on sugar and edible beets, and communicated his discoveries in scientific articles. In the summer of 1955, he was elected to be the director of the "Komunaras" collective in the Jonava district, but after one and a half years he withdrew due to failing health. He spent his final days in Kaunas, in the home of Sofija Kymantaitė-Čiurlionienė. His descendants chose a different professional route: his son Vladimir [the third Vladimir] became an architect, and in those footsteps went both of his sons, Konstantinas-Kastytis and Vytautas. His [the third Vladimir's] daughter Dalia Palukaitienė became a sculptor, and Kastytis' son Rokas Zubov became a pianist.

Although they had a deep impact on culture and the economy, written into history as a mutually supportive couple, Vladimir and Sofija Zubov were not able to save their personal happiness together. Vaclovas Bielskis (1870–1936), the brother of socialist Jonas Bielskis who'd taught Vladimir Zubov, returned to Šiauliai from working in the Ukraine in 1905. He was married to a Ukrainian, Vera Ušakovą (1877–1941) and had two daughters. Vaclovas Bielskis and Vladimir Zubov were acquainted from student days in Petersburg. In the recollection of General Jonas Bulota: "When I entered the military medical academy in Petersburg, I found a group of Lithuanian students there, led by Petras Vileišis. As I remember, the leaders among members of the group were men later prominent in our society: the engineer V. Bielskis, Vl. Zubov, a former major of Vilnius Kymantas, and others."[42]

Starting in 1906, Vaclovas was the administrator of Aleksandra Zubovienė's estate, which meant he often visited his old friend Zubov, and ... his wife Vera came into

---

[42] Dim. Div. Gen. Jonui Bulotai 85 metai // *Trimitas*, 1940, Nr. 16, p. 376.

Vladimir's awareness. In 1911, at Sofija's request, there was a divorce and the spouses never came back together after that. [Sofija was 51 years old; Vladimir was 49. -RS] Vladimir left the Ginkūnai estate, married Verą Bielskienė and went to live in Medemrodė. Various political people often came to visit him for advice. Vladas Požėla, who was forming a social-democratic party of Lithuania, offered him a place on the ballot for the organization, but the Count declined. He withdrew from politics entirely and immersed himself in farming.

Anticipating his imminent death, Vladimir Zubov asked that he be buried in a rye field and that the soil be left flat with no gravesite or monument. The Count died on June 23, 1933. [At the age of 71. -RS] Professor Steponas Kairys who attended the burial remembers: "His closest friends assembled, along with neighbors and estate workers. No delegations. Vladimir Zubov had said goodbye to all kinds of confessions long ago, therefore he was buried with no religious ceremony. That was his wish. He was buried at home, in the old Medemrodė cemetery. When his closest friends threw soil that they'd brought to scatter on the grave, a hundred-year-old oak tree and a piece of heavy granite were the only sentinels on the grave."[43] His second wife Vera Zubovienė had a large stone monument built for him. She herself was deported to Siberia in 1941 and died in exile. [She was 64 years old. -RS]

After the divorce, Sofija Bilevičiūtė-Zubovienė hosted Ginkūnai with her daughter Aleksandra, but when the First World War started, they retreated to Russia and lived in Crimea and Moscow. In Alupka in Crimea, in 1915,

---

[43] Steponas Kairys, *Lietuva budo*, Čikaga, 1957, p. 168.

Aleksandra Zubovaitė married Jonas Fledžinskas. Fledžinskas was active in the social-democratic movement. He was involved in revolutionary activities in 1905, and imprisoned. After that Vladimir Zubov hired him as an accountant on the estate. And that accountant fell in love with Aleksandra... Although Aleksandra's grandmother, the elder Countess Aleksandra Olsufjevaitė-Zubovienė had envisioned another husband for her grandchild and had summoned him to *Yasnaya Polyana* at the Tolstoy's, seeking to make a match, but the young Countess did not like the offered groom.[44]

After six years of friendship, Jonas Fledžinskas became the administrator of Ginkūnai. This is how he recalled his first visit to Ginkūnai, and the first meeting with Sofija Bilevičiūtė-Zubovienė: "A footman met me, led me to the cloakroom, took my coat and I entered the dining room. The lady of the house was there – a tall, plump, majestic lady, who was at the same time unpretentious and sophisticated, the extraordinary woman whom I would later call "Mother." From my very first introduction, I sensed a great rapport."[45]

When the family returned from Russia after the war, half of the Ginkūnai neoclassical-styled manor lay in ruins, a mess everywhere, and it required major renovation. The Germans had ruined most of the structures on the farm – barns, pig sty, granaries, mills, icehouse. They broke the agricultural equipment, carried away all the animals, and left only two horses that were useless for work. Countess Zubovienė and her daughter sheltered in Dabikinė for a

---

[44] Jonas Fledžinskas, *Atsiminimai,* Šiauliai, 1997, p. 39–40.
[45] Ten pat, p. 32.

while, taking over two rooms from the housekeepers. Then the Fledžinskas family with Sofija Zubovienė lived in Šiauliai, in a two-story house surrounded by the city garden, and when that was sold in order to build a teachers' seminary for the Education Ministry, they moved to a house on Kuršėnai Street.

Sofija Bilevičiūtė-Zubovienė and her offspring, Palanga, 1930

Standing, from left to right: grand-daughter Ona Zubovaitė-Oertelienė, son-in-law Jonas Fledžinskas, Sofija Bilevičiūtė-Zubovienė, her son Vladimir Zubov, grand-son Vladimir Zubov; sitting: daughter-in-law Ona Jakubauskaitė-Zubovienė, grand-son Jurgis Fledžinskas, daughter Aleksandra Zubovaitė-Fledžinskienė; kneeling, grand-children Marija Zubovaitė-Dementjevienė, Vytautas Fledžinskas, Aleksandra Fledžinskaitė-Kašubienė, Sofija Fledžinskaitė-Pempienė.

The first two grandchildren of Sofija were born in Šiauliai – Vytautas in 1919 and Sofija in 1920. Aleksandra and Jurgis came into the world after they'd returned to Ginkūnai, in 1923 and 1924. In Ginkūnai there enough rooms habitable for members of the family and numerous summer visitors. Sofija acquired a small farm near the estate managed by her son Dimitri, in Smiltynė, where she stayed occasionally, and in the summer, she brought all four grandchildren there. "Mother put a lot of work and energy into raising and educating the children," wrote Jonas Fledžinskas, "Her greatest joy was to help us raise them to be healthy, physically and spiritually. Mother's great intelligence, her gentle nature, patience and indulgence had a positive effect on the children around her."[46] Even though she was of a revered age, Sofija surprisingly quickly became very close to her daughter and son-in-law – she also learned the Lithuanian language and cultivated a Lithuanian spirit in the home. As Fledžinskas put it, "She worked to make a genuine Lithuanian home. She was with us all the time. She lived to take care of others."[47]

Although uniformed servants no longer took charge of the table on the estate, there were governesses and, of course, perfect music teachers. One Fledžinskas daughter, the famous artist and sculptor Aleksandra Fledžinskaitė-Kašuba remembers her grandmother sitting down in the early morning to play familiar Chopin etudes. In the summer, there was chamber music after dinner, when the whole family played – Aleksandra Zubovaitė-Fledžinskienė played the piano, her husband and children joined in with stringed

---

[46] Ten pat, p. 58.
[47] Ten pat, p. 59.

instruments. And in the winter, the mother, seating her four offspring on a sled in a row according to their age, slowly pulled them creaking through the snow in the moonlight.[48]

A few other facts and distinctive highlights punctuate Sofija Belevičiūtė-Zubovienė's later life: in 1926 President Kazys Grinius and a delegation from the Lithuanian Republic visited Ginkūnai. In 1929 Aleksandra Fledžinskienė and her mother founded an association called the "Ginkūnai Estate." In 1930 "Grandma" Sofija commemorated her seventieth birthday. The celebration was written up in the press with a tribute: "Countess Zubovienė – a generous soul, a great intellect, a highly-educated woman, whose considerable personal talents were put to work for our nation's rebirth [...]. Although she celebrates turning seventy years old, old age has not yet touched her soul: she actively thinks about our social and political life, a new Lithuania and a world-class literature; she is raising her grandchildren in a nationalist spirit, hoping for and anticipating their contributions to our country."[49]

---

[48] Aleksandra Kašuba, Moteris dykumoje // *Respublika*, 2013 06 14, p. 22.
[49] L. Tomkytė, Garbingos sukaktuvės // *Šiaures Lietuva*, 1930 07 18, p. 3.

Sofija Bilevičiūtė-Zubovienė

Sofija Bilevičiūtė-Zubovienė left this world in 1932. [She was 72 years old. - RS] Wanting to put her to rest nearby, members of the family had her buried in Žuvininkai cemetery on the edge of Ginkūnai. Standing on the veranda of Ginkūnai, you can see her gravesite and her cross. In the newspaper "Šiaurės Lietuva" [Northern Lithuania], after the printed obituary were the following words: "On the 9th of June, Countess Sofija Zubovienė died suddenly in the early morning. On the 11th of June at 10 a.m. in the morning, she'll be buried at her estate Graužiai, in the Catholic cemetery. A funeral mass will be held the same day at 8 a.m. in the morning at Cathedral of St. Peter and Paul in Šiauliai. Countess S. Zubovienė was a teacher in higher education and a writer. She contributed much to our people during the times of oppression. Her gracious soul and many impressive contributions to our Fatherland will bring many people to her funeral. Let there be Light on her for eternity."[50]

In 1940, the Ginkūnai estate was nationalized, and the estate property was designated a Soviet cooperative. The Fledžinskas family who were the estate administrators were not subject to deportation. Jonas Fledžinskas died in Skaudvilė.

From the prior Zubov estate in Ginkūnai remained only a rebuilt residence and two original buildings – the storage house built at the beginning of the 20th Century and the dairy beside it. Gone were the building that housed workers, large trees, and flower gardens. There is a gymnasium in Ginkūnai in the name of Sofija and Vladimir Zubov, and in 1985, a museum was set up inside.

Sofija Bilevičiūtė-Zubovienė's gravesite
"Here lies ... Died in Ginkūnai
1932 June 9th, 72 years old

It is hard to overstate the contribution of the Zubov family to Lithuania's culture and economy. They lived in a time when most Lithuanian landowners abandoned their property and entertained

---

[50] Mirė Graf. Sofija Zubovienė // Šiaures Lietuva, 193 06 12, p. 1.

themselves abroad, while the Zubovs diligently tended to their model farms. While other landowners turned to Poland and became alienated from the culture, the Zubovs not only got closer to local people and learned the Lithuanian language, but for generations over more than 200 years ploughed Lithuanian soil. Despite persecution by the government, they rallied Lithuanian and nationalist gatherings and helped expand the national Lithuanian press during Russification. As nobility, they rejected titles and consciously turned to the common people: they encouraged and provided for the poor, concerned themselves with the education of the young, intervened in the persecution of social activists by wartime officials, and supported life in the Šiauliai region financially and spiritually. After two centuries, Vytautas Kubilius writes: "Sending in the Zubovs – that was the only great gift of Catherine II to Lithuania."

The readers of Sofija Bilevičiūtė-Zubovienė's novel "Laimė" [Happiness] gave it a cool reception,[51] and it barely had time to get a fair reading and a review. Will the work be perceived differently in our time and in the Lithuanian language?

It is one more fruit among the cultural legacies of leading women in Lithuania. It is a footprint on the path walked by champions of our country. The story reveals a side of a couple's private life together and tells us that maybe you can be happy working for the good of others.

---

[51] Jonas Fledžinskas, *Atsiminimai*, Šiauliai, 1997, p. 59.

Story of the Translations:
From Polish to Lithuanian
by Jolanta Kriuniene

Ian Vorres

Sofijos Bilevičiūtės-Zubovienės novel "Laimė" is one of four books our publishing house *Verba vera* issued about estates and landowners. All four books explore themes of the period. The individuals involved were not only contemporaries, they also knew each other: the Dukes Vasilčikovs were people close to the Tsar, the Zubovs and Vasilčikovs knew each other, and Vasilčikovs and Vakseli were not only neighbors, they were also distant relatives. Two of the books helped me discover a third—the book "Laimė" lost for nearly one hundred years.

The first book was issued in 2013: Ian Vorres' "Paskutinioji didžioji kunigaikštienė" (a translation of *The Last Great Dutchess*). This was a memoir of Olga Alexandrovna, the sister of Russia's Tsar Nicholar II, dictated to her friend Ian Vorres (1924-2015) when she lived in Canada. The book made such a great impression on me that I translated it, we published it, and I travelled to St. Petersburg to visit the Tsar's palace. Immediately after that, on invitation from the book's author, I flew to Greece to meet Ian Vorres—

the owner of an enormous museum of art in the suburb Paiania, East Attica, near Athens, who was also a collector and patron of the arts. I corresponded with him frequently while preparing the book. Meeting him was wonderful.

Baroness Olga Vakselyte

While I was writing the press release for the Tsar's sister's memoirs captured by Ian Vorres, I read a lot about the lives of Russian Tsars. In one book, a particular event caught my interest: when the Tsar's family retreated from St. Petersburg and hid in Crimea during the revolution. With them were the Dukes Vasilčikov, the owners of the Jurbarke estate. I'd never heard of them before. I wanted to know more. The same summer, when Ian Vorres' book was published, I drove to Jurbarkas and visited the Vasilčikov estate museum. While chatting with the director of the museum, she offered: "Are you interested in estates? Perhaps you'd like to meet Baroness Olga Vakselytė, the owner of the Veliuona estate. She happens to be there right now, visiting from Canada."

Right after I got back from Jurbarkas I dropped in at Veliuona. I told the Baroness that we'd just published the memoir of the Tsar's sister. "Oh, I knew her!" she exclaimed. "We'd just arrived in Canada when I met her. She was old, by then, and quite down-to-earth." That's how my relationship with Baroness Olga Vakselyte-Larson began.

In Veliuona with Olga Vakselyte-Larson

Every year, in the summer, Olga Vakselyte flew from Canada to Veliuona, the estate owned by her father which she had reclaimed. I took my family to visit the estate a few times, and sometimes she visited me in Kaunas. Lady Olga loved to tell stories about the old days and her parents and grandparents. I learned that her father was born and raised in Romainiai near Kaunas. I got interested in the history of estates in Romainiai. I dove into archival manuscripts. Step by step I'd collected material for a monograph on the Romainiai estates. This work *"Romainių dvareliai—išlikęs ir išnykęs"* [The Estates of Romainiai—the remained one and the vanished one] was written over three years and published in 2016.

Dukes Vasilcikova

Still writing the monograph about Romainiai, I didn't
forget my interest in the Vasilčikovs. The Dukes Vasilčikovs
distinguished themselves as people with literary talents: the
last owner of Jurbarkas, Ilarionas Sergejevičius, his wife
Lidija Leonidovna Viazemskaja and their two daughters
Tatjana and Marija wrote memoirs. I decided to translate the
memoirs of Marija Vasilčikova into Lithuanian and to give
Lithuanian readers her book, "*Berlyno dienoraščiai 1940–1945*"
(a translation of *The Berlin Diaries 1940–1945*). The book was
published in 2014. Because the Vasilčikova's were not well
known in Lithuania, I started to write an in-depth article
about this noble family, which I inserted at the end of the
book. Again, I researched material for the article in the
archives, in museums, in old newspapers before the war, and
interviewed long-time residents of Jurbarkas.

Dalia Palukaitiene

Now it occurred to me to knock on the door of Sofija Kymantaitės-Čiurlionienės home in Kaunas. I knew that when the Vasilčikovs lost their estate Jurbarkas after the first World War, they lived in Kaunas during 1934-1937, renting a flat of five rooms in S.K. Čiurlionienė's house. I didn't know who lived there now but I trusted that they might hear me out and possibly tell me something about the Dukes Vasilčikovs. M.K. Čiurlionis' granddaughter Dalia Palukaitienė kindly took me in and shared information for my article.

During one visit, I asked Dalia if she wanted me to publish something about her family's history. Not the same day but another time when I was getting up to leave, Dalia Palukaitienė suddenly opened a small book case in her living room. She pulled out a little book with a brown cover. She gave it to me and said, "Here, read this. If you like it, you can publish it." She was quiet for a bit, and then she added, "I would love to know what's written in here!" I took a quick look and saw that the book was in Polish. My first thought was: "How on earth did she know I can read Polish?"

We can count only a few readers in Kaunas who know Polish, these days. I know Polish from childhood on. Also, I'd spent years working intensively in the archives, reading documents written in old Polish and Russian languages. But Dalia did not know about that. That's why, when she said, "Read this!" I got a queasy feeling and it sounded as if some kind of message from the beyond was telling me to take on this task. "Has anyone you know read the book?" I asked, given that she herself couldn't read Polish. She said, "They read it. But there's no one left to tell me about it."

I read the novel and liked it. I took on the translation and finished it in four months. When Dalia Palukaitienė read the translation, her first words were: "You know, that's exactly the way it was! My father told me about it." After that the two of us edited my translation. It was just like Sofijos Kymantaitės-Čiurlionienė's salons held on Saturdays, between the wars. The

Dalia Palukaitienė, talk in library, 2015

novel was published in the summer of 2015.

Only when the book was published did I find out how Dalia Palukaitienė found this book that had gone missing more than one hundred years. Here's what she told readers, during a presentation of the book in the Kaunas public library: She knew about the existence of the novel even as a child. Family members talked about it. But they had no idea that the only existing copy was sitting... in their home library. In the year just past, Dalia was organizing her grandmother Sofijos Kymantaitės-Čiurlionienės literary legacy, browsing among books in the family libary, sorting old papers. And so, among books belonging to her grandmother Ona Jakubauskaitė (her father's mother), she found a little book stuck deep in a bookcase. She opened it. It was her great-grandmother Sofija Bilevičiūtės-Zubovienė's "Laimė"!

Story of the Translations:

From Lithuanian to English

by Ruta Sevo

Family diaspora – forced flight

Less than ten years after both Zubovs died, a golden age of Lithuanian independence came to an end. The period between 1918 and 1940 was a time of peace, prosperity, and nation-building. Lithuanian nationalism flourished and expressed itself in economic development, urbanization, and cultural discovery. A Lithuanian identity and culture rose in the freedom to publish and educate in the Lithuanian language. Folk festivals and libraries did not have to be secret.

The catastrophic disruption that is war arrived suddenly with first the invasion of Russian soldiers (after June 15, 1940), then German (after June 22, 1941), and then Russian again (after July, 1944). The Russians targeted upper classes for elimination, and their method was deportation to Siberia to camps where the most likely outcome was a slow death from cold, starvation, brutal outdoor work, and disease.[52] The Germans murdered nearly all of the 200,000 Jews in Lithuania. With the return of a Russian occupation in 1944, upper classes in Lithuania knew that their days were numbered—they'd seen the lists compiled from the prior short occupation.

Three of four Zubov grandchildren fled for their lives, on twenty-four hours' notice, leaving the country and eventually emigrating to Australia and the USA. Several carried their first babies out with them. The Zubov's daughter, Countess Aleksandra and her husband Jonas Fledzinskas and one of their sons were spared deportation by the grace of a friend who had the ability to take their names off the lists for deportation. They retreated to the Fledzinskas' home village of Skaudvile, to live modestly with a cow, chickens, and a garden.

Vladimir Zubov's second wife Vera did not escape deportation; she had married a noble and entered the category of people targeted by the Soviets. She was sent to Siberia in 1941 and died in exile at the age of 64 years.

The Ginkunai manor house had been taken over by Soviet officers, then German officers, and then Soviet officers again. Under the Soviet occupation, the land was polluted with oil spills (according to some surviving family members), and eventually there were some reparations paid, once Lithuania was independent again. Now it is a compound including an office building, a school, and a small museum.

---

[52] It is estimated that 300,000 total were deported. See https://en.wikipedia.org/wiki/Soviet_deportations_from_Lithuania See also the young-adult novel by Ruta Sepetys, *Between Shades of Grey* (2012), Speak.

Only recently have books come out, many of them self-published, about the invasions, the flights, and life under Soviet occupation.[53] Lithuania became independent in February, 1991, and emigres were free to return after that (if they'd done well enough to bear the cost of a significant trip), to visit relatives for the first time in forty-seven years, and to digest the traumatic separation.

Ginkunai was purchased in 1805 by Platon Zubov, the recipient of "the economy of Siauliai" by Empress Catherine II. After Platon's death in 1822, his son Dimitri (1764-1836) inherited the farms settled in Siauliai, making Ginkunai the center of the estate's economic activity. His son Nikolajus Zubov (1801-1871) was the Zubov who built a number of manor houses. He married an Italian-French Countess and had four children. One of those children, another Nikolajus (1832-1898) mostly lived in Siaulai in Didziadvaris and became a well-known public figure in the area: a noble leader of the region and after 1878 the leader of the Kaunas province also.

That means these Zubovs (Sofija and Vladimir) were the fifth generation to own the estate Ginkunai (with numbers of manor houses) and enjoy it for their entire lifetimes. The sixth generation, Aleksandra Zubovaite-Fledzinskiene (1891-1961), was forced off the estate (at age

---

[53] Mark Wyman, *DPs: Europe's Displaced Persons, 1945-1951* (Cornell U Press, 1989). *Ellen Cassedy, We Are Here: Memories of the Lithuanian Holocaust* (U of Nebraska Press, 2012). Ona Algminiene, *The Crimson Blight* (1968, translated to English 2014). *Julija Sukys, Epistolophilia: Writing the Life of Ona Simaite* (U of Nebraska Press, 2012). "The Invisible Front" movie (2014)

53). Her youngest child, Jurgis Fledzinskas, was 20 years old, studying music. The rest were already off to university.

The details of the dispersal of other members of Aleksandra's generation, for example, her brother Vladimir Zubov (1887-1959) and his descendants is unknown to me, except that Vladimir's children survived and lived in Kaunas, and some emigrated to the USA. Apparently, the youngest Vladimir Zubov (grandson of the first Vladimir) was deported, and Jonas Fledzinskas paid the Russians to let him return to Lithuania.[54]

A Zubov family history of about 136 years and six generations was violently disrupted. The theme after 1940 was physical survival, and psychological survival of terror, violence, trauma, poverty, and forced migration to foreign lands.

Sofija's granddaughter Sofija Fledzinskaite-Pempiene (1920-2013) fled with her husband Eric Pempe. Since he spoke perfect German, they rode some of the 600 miles in trucks full of German soldiers who were also fleeing the second Russian invasion. Like others, they found shelter in German farms and towns. He risked his life to steal potatoes, evading German Shepherd guard dogs. My mother gave birth in a clinic about 100 miles south of Berlin, in the American Sector, on May 7th, 1945, a day of world-wide euphoria. Then they moved into Displaced Person camps. In post-war Europe, there were severe food shortages, vast destruction of infrastructure, and hostility and distrust between most ethnic and language groups. My family's story is a close parallel to a good written account.[55] Sofija B. Zuboviene's other

---

[54] Per conversation with my mother, 2009.
[55] Edward R. Janusz, *Fading Echoes from the Baltic Shores* (2012)

granddaughter Aleksandra Kasuba also described her journey.[56]

The human toll of World War II is beyond our credulity now. About 20 million people were displaced after World War II—refugees wandering, homeless, in some cases returning to their former homes only to be shot by the new occupants. But those lost is also beyond comprehension: one estimate is: "Over 60 million people were killed, which was about 3% of the 1940 world population."[57]

To help vacate the displaced person camps that persisted nearly five years in Europe, the USA opened its quotas in 1949 to allow large numbers of immigrants to enter. Thanks to the generosity of America, my family was blessed and given a chance at a new beginning.

This was not the beginning of an easy life. Many professionals did not speak English and were not qualified for professional work in America. Medical doctors had to pass exams in English, or, they were allowed to practice in mental institutions. My parents were teachers who would have had to renew their credentials. They already knew the English language. They arrived with nothing in New York City and cleaned office buildings on the night shift. Then my father got a job working in a coal mine in the middle of Utah. He took correspondence courses and got a white-collar job as a drafting engineer. Meanwhile, without the benefit of contraceptives, two more children were born and had to be supported.

In spite of the difficulties, a new life in America was one of the best opportunities to be had. By the time my mother

---

[56] Aleksandra Kasuba, *On the Way to America* (2010)
[57] https://en.wikipedia.org/wiki/World_War_II_casualties

passed at the age of 93, she owned her home, had superb medical care, supported several sons, and enjoyed the comfort and beauty of a home full of favorite things in Seattle, Washington, a place reminiscent of the Baltic. However, my family lived in social isolation, far from family and with few American friends. The trauma and effort of seventy years "in exile," navigating a foreign language and culture and climbing out of poverty with five children, left her tired and philosophical, if not sad. I might even say that my father suffered what we now call post-traumatic stress syndrome—unable to forget and forgive the atrocities he'd witnessed.

I leave it to others to describe the traumatic stress and tolls of living under Soviet occupation for forty-seven years. There are stories very close to home about deportees (many professionals) who were allowed to return from Siberia after many years of suffering but were denied access to education and jobs. They often moved back to live with relatives, in broken health, in some cases making a life and even finding success in spite of the adversity.

The main point of this short family history is to explain that the family heritage of the "golden years" of power and privilege, and nobility, were over. We are now entering the tenth generation of Platon Zubov's descendants. Four generations have followed in America with émigré elders who might have remained completely silent about the past and the family, due to trauma. (This type of silence has been reported in many memoirs of holocaust survivors also—the silence of unspeakable experiences.)

The cohesion of the family was lost in geographic and cultural dispersion. Besides silent first-generation elders, language is a barrier. The Soviet occupation shut down all personal communication for forty-seven years. A few photographs were carried out, and new ones could not be sent. Long distance phone calls were prohibitively expensive, and travel even after 1991 was a luxury financially struggling immigrants could not afford. Later generations married Americans and may not even identify as "Lithuanian-American." Poverty alone was a big barrier to our ability to reconnect.

My father died in February of 1990, an exact year before Lithuania regained independence. He saw the trend and realized it meant that a personal and political nightmare was possibly over. However, he was in no position to celebrate by jumping on a plane.

Before the Internet, tracking and staying in touch with displaced family was nearly impossible. The people most interested and those who knew where to look were busy putting food on the table. Long-distance phone calls were still too costly. There were no tools for family genealogy and family history near at hand. At this time, I can safely say that most of the family in generations seven-eight-nine (since Platon Zubov) hardly know who is a member and where they might be found. I estimate 150-200 people. (Generation ten is the one in early childhood now.) A deep family identity and sense of connection was lost in the catastrophic disruption.

That explains to me why the books are coming out now. Lithuanian independence in 1991 opened the country to visitors and intensive, free communication. The proliferation of the Internet ("universal, global access") starting in the late 1990's[58] made it possible to find information more easily. Now, we can tour Ginkunai using Google Earth, read the local Siauliai newspaper, recover genealogies in multiple

---

[58] See https://en.wikipedia.org/wiki/History_of_Google

sites, find family through DNA tests, and "friend" our scattered family members on Facebook if not talk to them live using Skype. We can use Google Translate to break the language barrier.

It is possible to create a road map to extended family and pay them a visit. But now the barriers are personal interest, skills, and time. The family widely extended across continents are strangers. What ties us together across life styles, values, culture, and language, except DNA?

Fledzinskas legacy

My grandfather, Jonas Fledzinskas (1885-1965), was also a leader in free Lithuania, carrying on the Zubov traditions of agricultural development, export development, philanthropy and community leadership.[59] His mother-in-law, Sofija Zuboviene, lived with him and her daughter Aleksandra, admired him and helped raise his four children, who arrived within a period of five years (1919-1924).

He wrote a memoir in 1958-1959 (during the Soviet occupation of Lithuania), which came into the hands of the family abroad. His children in the USA approved and financially sponsored its publication by the Ausros Museum in Siaulai, in 1997.[60] Precious copies were given to his

---

[59] https://lt.wikipedia.org/wiki/Jonas_Fledzinskas (need to request a translation for English)

[60] Fledzinskas, Jonas (1997) *Atsiminimai: medziaga istorija.* Siauliai, Lietuva: Siauliu "Ausros" Muziejus. Redaktoriu Kolegija: Eugenija Jovaisaite and Eugeija Raguckiene. Dailininke: Vita Andruliene. Leidybos Vadove: Virginija Siuscience. 119 pages paperback

American grandchildren, many of whom could not read the Lithuanian language.

Once I retired in 2006, I embarked on a translation for the sake of American family who could not read the book, and myself. My knowledge of Lithuanian was at the level of "kitchen talk," but I had seriously learned four other languages in the meantime (German, French, Bengali, and Sanskrit), had translated Bengali novels, and even received one of 3 nationally-awarded PEN Translation Fellows in 1973 (for Bengali). I was comfortable with dictionaries and difficult language analysis (with two years of deciphering Sanskrit verse).

I'd never met my grandfather, due to lack of funds and the barrier imposed by the Soviet occupation for forty-seven years. He wrote a few letters to his grandchildren in America. Mine came during my last year in high school and first year in college (1963-1964). At the time, I was bombarded with the pressures of getting accepted to college, leaving home and succeeding in a high-pressured private college. Writing in Lithuanian was horribly difficult, lacking a dictionary or a native speaker at my shoulder. There was no room in my brain. His main message to me was: "Learn the language." I was deep in German language classes. I'd bought books to teach myself Greek and Italian. Lithuanian was the last thing I had room for.

As it turned out, I spend a college year abroad in Germany. I was in Tubingen by the end of summer, 1965, and made it as far as Berlin in 1966. I crossed through Check-point Charlie and spent a day in East Berlin even though there were rumors that the Soviets would keep you if they figured out you were born in East Germany (as I was). (They did not keep me.)

He died on March 1st, 1965, just weeks before I boarded the QE II to cross the Atlantic Ocean. It was forbidden to travel to Lithuania at that time, so the idea was completely out of my mind. The wall of Soviet rule was a tall, dark, impenetrable Iron Curtain. We had to forget Lithuania existed. As if your whole family and its history were in prison, forever. It's a tragedy of my life that political barriers, language and timing made our meeting impossible, and a few years of potential correspondence were nearly impossible due to my stage of life. I answered two of his letters in childish, broken Lithuanian, which he was pretty excited to receive.

In 2006, I travelled to Vilnius and installed myself in a tiny, unpretentious room in a hotel that was a former convent, Hotel Domus Maria. After the purchase of a dictionary three inches thick, I persevered for ten days. Two of Jonas Fledzinskas' children in America corrected my English draft: his son Vytautas (my uncle) and his daughter Sofija (my mother).

The result of the translation was a small self-published book, called *Memories of family and estate: Lithuania in the early 1900's*.[61] It was published as both a printed paperback and as an ebook, and made available commercially (with no royalty built in). My expectation was that its main readership would be family members (all

---

[61] Jonas Fledzinskas (1885-1995), 2010, English translation by Ruta Pempe Sevo with Vytautas Fledzinskas and Sophie Pempe.

those strangers!), but in fact soon about fifty people worldwide had purchased copies.

The reason I bring this up is that my grandfather's memoir became an auspicious link in the chain of events leading me to Sofia Zubov's novel.

Swedish sisters

In 2014, I received an email from a woman in Sweden who had found Jonas Fledzinskas' memoir online, making a random search related to her family's history in Lithuania. Her parents, like mine, were reluctant to talk about their past in the country, and she was eager to fill in some blanks.

It seems her grandfather, a Swede, worked on the Ginkunai estate (1924-1940) as an inspector and consultant on modern farming methods. He married a local Lithuanian girl and had every intention of staying in Lithuania. His wife's mother was a maid in the Fledzinskas household. They lived in a nice brick house in Gruzdziai and socialized often with the Fledzinskas family.

The two families were so close that Sofija Zuboviene "almost adopted" her maid's family, watching out for the education of the children in the family. The Swedish grandfather and mine were so close that hers named his first and only son "Vilius Jonas," which is not a Swedish name. A wedding gift from the Zubovs was a pair of enameled, silver napkin-holders with the inscriptions "W.Z 1909" and "Z.Z. 1909." [Wlodzimierz Zubov and Zofija Zubov, Polish versions of their names]

When the Germans invaded in 1941, they systematically took control over the locals, including noting the status of individual citizens. The Swedish inspector was advised that he could stay in Lithuania and in that case, he would be treated like a Russian citizen (and that was not very good, since he was a professional in close association with noble landowners), or, he could leave the country. My Swedish friend has a certificate written in German, signed by Fledzinskas, stating "Er verlies Litauen auf eigenen Wunch." [He leaves Lithuania by choice.] In fact, the Swede was given 48 hours to quit the country. They left for Poland, trusting all their money and valuables to the Swedish consul in Vilnius. They never saw any of it again, leaving a life-long bitterness toward his native country, to the extent that the inspector's Lithuanian wife declined to speak much Swedish.

The Swede's wife's Lithuanian relatives did not fare well after the Russians invaded, getting deported and dying in exile. It was a tragic end to their charmed life on farms in the Siauliai region: living on the estate with best friends and engaging in highly productive collaborations in agricultural research and operations.

Back to 2014. The Swedish woman and her sister spoke excellent English, but no Lithuanian. We planned a "roots visit" together in the summer of 2015. We hired an English-speaking guide, stayed the Hotel Domus Maria in Vilnius (again, for me), and drove to Siauliai and the surroundings. The few days' tour was intensely emotional as we spoke to contacts, looked at photos, walked through forest paths to hidden gravesites, and imagined the lost past. A story of our tour was published in *Lithuanian Heritage* magazine.[62]

We had in common a great fascination for the relationship between the grandfathers, and also the relationship between the elderly Sofia Zubov and the maid, who was the Swedish sisters' grandmother.

While in Siauliai, I met with someone who'd corresponded with me earlier: DS. We were in town for two days. The Swedish sisters spoke no Lithuanian and DS spoke no English, leaving me to translate our small talk, so they met with him only once. The second day, however, he brought me copies of *Laime*, the recently published novel by Sofia Zubov translated into Lithuanian.

It was a serendipitous, shocking moment in time: a secret novel unknown to us by the historical woman whom

---

[62] Ruta Sevo, "Lietuva Trip Report: Zubovas Family Legacy." *Lithuanian Heritage*, May/June 2016, vol 4 (S3), pp. 14-17.

we were in fervent pursuit, which had been lost for nearly one hundred years. After one hundred years, a book that appeared in Lithuanian book stores only two months before our visit!

In retrospect, there were mentions of the novel in Jonas Fledzinskas' memoir and in my aunt Aleksandra Kasuba's memoir[63]. But not a single relative of mine spoke of its existence to me; it was part of the silent family history.

So, who was DS and why did I meet up with him in Siauliai?

DS & DNA

Late in 2009, I received an email from Lithuania from DS, who sought genealogical information about the Zubovs. He wrote, in Lithuanian, that he'd had a son, and was interested in making a family tree for him. Particularly, he was chasing a rumor that his grandmother (born in 1910) was a love child whose father was Vladimir Zubov.

We both used Google Translate to help us read the emails, on both sides.

DS succeeded in building out a family tree of his own family and the Zubovs back possibly twenty generations into the royalty of Italy, France, as well as Russia, with photographs and dates. It seems to me that his staggering effort was really a search for truth and identity. The charts were a boon to our scattered family, and he wasn't even sure he was related.

---

[63] Aleksandra Kasuba, *Child Ticking* (2001). NY: Writer's Club Press.

His grandmother, born in 1910, was well-provided. Her mother had a modest house north of Ginkunai, with a "pseudo-house-husband" in residence for protection or respectability or whatever (we'll never know). At the time of the birth, the mother of this child was twenty-three years old and possibly a maid at Ginkunai. Vladimir was forty-eight at the time and still married to Sofija but possibly in love with his second wife Vera already.

The love child went on to have seven children, and DS's family tree branching from her included nearly forty people. Lithuania is a small country, and the Siauliai region even smaller, especially around 1910. It wasn't easy to disappear into a large population. However, I imagine class differences narrowed the scope of social interactions and possibly rumors.

At the time of our communication (2009), DNA testing was just beginning to be available to individuals at a reasonable cost and it was still an esoteric pursuit.[64] Since then, the trend to pursue genealogy and family history has exploded, bringing down the cost and the options for types of analysis.[65] Searching online, we found a company based in London that could do paternity verification within two generations (that is, determine if two people had a common grandparent). (Technically, an "autosomal blood relationship test," for about $400.)

With some reluctance, my mother volunteered to swab her cheek. DS had an uncle do the same. In few months, the results were in: "We can state that the possibility of the two

---

[64] For current sources see
http://isogg.org/wiki/List_of_DNA_testing_companies
[65] http://www.pbs.org/weta/finding-your-roots/resources/

submitted samples to be related with each other is 99.97093%."

DS was ecstatic. He'd settled one of his roots for his son, himself, and nearly forty other people in his family tree. He could now "own" the genealogical work he'd done—these were indeed his ancestors, with proof. He donated charts to the Ausros Museum in Siauliai (which has archives on the Zubovs). He biked to the gravesites and tended to the weeds overgrowing them. He campaigned to get a park and schools in Siauliai renamed, since the Zubov names had been erased during the Soviet occupation. He campaigned for articles about the Zubov legacy in the Siauliai newspaper.

A few members of my family were not thrilled about the exposure of a family secret that in normal times might be shameful and dishonorable, even though the event was one hundred years old. Clearly, however, the secret was well kept. In fact, I asked DS why he thought the secret had been kept so long. His own mother told him the story for the first time only as she was dying in 2008. The illicit daughter (his grandmother) had come to maturity during the Soviet occupation. It was dangerous to speak of any ties to nobility—the consequence was deportation and probable death. It seems that the forces in favor of secrecy might have been a combination of shame and extreme political danger.

I can safely say that love children have been born since the beginning of human history. The consequences, to the mother and the child, depend on the society and culture, and class, and whether the mother can sustain a life outside the supports of a marital relationship, especially financial support.

Tolstoy himself had a child with a serf before he married his wife (in 1862, named Sophia) and then proceeded to have thirteen children (one of whom was named Alexandra). (In those days, a number of them did not survive. Only eight of Tolstoy's children survived childhood.) The love child was revealed in his wife's diaries.[66]

Here's a story of his son:

"Ivan Shtref: Is it true that Tolstoy had many illegitimate children? Did any of them become writers?

Pavel Basinsky: We can only say with certainty that Tolstoy had one illegitimate child – a son by a married peasant woman, Aksinya Bazykina, born before his marriage to Sofia Andreyevna (once married, he remained faithful to his wife). The son lived at Yasnaya Polyana, was even the village prefect for a while, then served as coachman for Tolstoy's older sons, but later drank himself to death.

Unfortunately, this was the usual fate for illegitimate children of aristocracy. They saw themselves as superior to their environment (what with their noble fathers), but had to remain where they were born for there was no way to legitimize illegitimate children. Russia was an Orthodox – not a secular – state, where only children born after a church wedding, christened and entered into a special church book could be considered legitimate. So Tolstoy's son could not have become his legitimate offspring even if his father

---

[66] https://en.wikipedia.org/wiki/Leo_Tolstoy

wanted him to. Furthermore, Aksinya had a husband, and Tolstoy's wife Sofia was a very jealous woman."[67]

Another famous case of an elite landowner and leader and his inappropriate and secret liaison with a slave (not a "serf"), in America is Thomas Jefferson. Allegations that Thomas Jefferson was consorting with his slave Sally Hemmings were already in play in 1802. DNA evidence in 1998 (e.g., almost two hundred years later) found that at least one and maybe six of her children were fathered by Jefferson but this was disputed and extensively analyzed.[68]

According to DS, the child fathered by Vl. Zubov out of wedlock grew up to become the mother of seven and had a difficult life due to a difficult husband. One of her uncles escaped Stalin's murderous campaigns by taking himself into hiding in Siberia. Life in occupied Lithuania was not easy for anyone.

Some say that Vladimir Zubov was already living separately from Sofija in 1909 (moving to the manor in Medemrode), although they did not formally divorce until 1911. The year he divorced, Vladimir married his second wife Vera Usakova-Bielskiene (1877-1941). (She was 34 and he was 51.)

If we assume that some of the values expressed by the fictional character Elvyra are the same values held by Sofija Zubov, we can imagine that she would find a love child abhorrent. The character says many times that marriage is a

---

[67]

http://rbth.com/articles/2012/04/07/a_prominent_literary_critic_reveals_to lstoys_mystery_15270.html

[68] https://www.monticello.org/site/plantation-and-slavery/thomas-jefferson-and-sally-hemings-brief-account

necessary social construct for the optimal socialization of children, and that the very survival of the species is at stake in this adaptive, evolutionary social structure. The character Elvyra might have found a love child the last straw in a troubled relationship—a violation of the natural order.

There are surprising parallels between things described in the novel and events in real life that *followed* the novel in sequence by many years. First, the novel was published in 1902 but the couple did not separate and divorce until 1909-1911. According to their granddaughter,[69] the original ending of the novel had the couple separate. Sofija Zubov rewrote the ending to have the couple tearfully reunite. Possibly she rewrote the ending to appease her husband. But in real life, she was right: their relationship did not survive his "free love" philosophy.

A second parallel regards Vladimir's second wife. For example, in the story, the husband Stephonas has a woman friend who is married, and she is interested in him as a second husband. (The character Elvyra accuses her of "seeking an upgrade.") The woman says to him: "You keep your sons, and I'll keep my daughters." The novel was published in 1902. In reality, Vladimir Zubov met his second wife Vera, a married woman with two daughters, in 1905, and married her in 1911. (By then his children were grown.) She did indeed "get an upgrade" by becoming a Countess Zubov. (And she inherited the Medemrode estate.)

According to granddaughter Aleksandra Kasuba, the family was involved in the decision to divorce:

"The divorce [was of] great concern to the family. Before approving such a move, hardly heard of at the

---

[69] Per conversation with Aleksandra Kasuba.

time, Grandfather's siblings held a meeting and after discussing the matter, set a condition: unless he divided his property before filing for divorce, the family would proclaim him insane to secure the children's rightful inheritance. Grandfather split his holdings into three parts (Grandmother refusing her share), and after changing religion from Greek Orthodox to Calvinism, took a second wife, who had also divorced her husband and had two grown daughters."[70]

As I stated under "Family Diaspora" above, around 1940 the Zubov family heritage of "golden years of power and privilege," and nobility, were over. The family is now fragmented and scattered across continents. Many living outside of Lithuania, among three generations "in exile" now, are total strangers to each other.

It is hard to imagine any family reunion or council of family elders who might convene and accuse DS or me of tampering with the family honor. It seems to me that the veneration of people who have royal titles but who have no "power and privilege" is shallow in the USA now. It also seems to me that there is still some cachet in having a title in Lithuania, even though "Count so-and-so" may not be in a position of "power and privilege." In Lithuania, there seems to be historical respect for nobility and their contributions, especially for nation-building during Lithuanian independence between the wars. The title "Count" does not convey to the next generation through daughters, so it is mostly men who might use it. In America, using the title may be considered eccentric and curious, and even pretentious,

---

[70] Aleksandra Kasuba, *Child Ticking* (2001). NY: Writers Club Press. p. 83.

like addressing someone as "Doctor" who is not a medical doctor.

I don't think anyone in America or in Lithuania is going to stop inviting us to grand parties at their grand manor house on a large estate.

The exchange with DS that led to a DNA test gave him a truth he'd been seeking for a long time, and a new identity as a real descendant of Vladimir Zubov. In effect, by sponsoring a DNA test, I gave him a meaningful piece of his family heritage. When he gave me a copy of Sofija's novel, he gave me a meaningful piece of my family heritage back.

Translation

After receiving a copy of *Laime*, I immediately obtained the rights to write an English translation, communicating with Jolanta Kriuniene. I was eager to know how it read in English, and I knew the Swedish sisters and my family in America were highly interested. For anyone researching family history, a novel is a rare bonus find. Even though it's fiction, it offers a sense for the mind of an ancestor—what was on their mind and what characters and plot they chose to include in a story, what personality is in the "voice" of the narrative.

My translation work did not begin for over a year. When I told Jolanta Kriuniene, who had put so much work into the Polish-to-Lithuanian translation and an essay on the Zubovs, that I was looking for a translator who could verify my drafts, she said, "Why not me?" It turned out that English translation is among her skills. Thus our stories converged again.

An Abbreviated Timeline of SBZ's Life

By Ruta Sevo

1860   **Birth SBZ :** SBZ is born in Kaunas and spends her childhood at the Aušbikavis estate, near Raseinių in the Taurages region. To Count Hipolitas Bilevičias (1822-1901) and Elena Daugirdaitė-Bilevičienė (1841-1940). Elena is from the Klišių estate near Viekšniu.

   SBZ is the eldest of nine children (five boys and four girls). She often travels abroad with her parents.

1862   **Birth VZ :** Vladimir Zubov (1962-1933) is born on Didžiadvaria estate in Šiauliai on March 18. To Nikolajus Nikolajevičius Zubov (1832-1898) and Aleksandra Olssufjevaitė-Zubovienė (1840-1913).

   He is one of four children: Vladimir, Mariją, Olgą, and Dimitri.

1869   **Girls' Hostel :** Nikolajus gives annual funding for a girls' hostel which becomes gymnasium for girls in 1898.

1872   **Move :** Sofia's parents move their family to Vilnius. Sofia studies in the Emilija Vrublevska Polish school.

1874   **Library :** Left-leaning students create a secret, illegal Lithuanian library, stored in Didžidvaria manor. Issues of the illegal newspaper Aušros is distributed through it to the market.

1874 **Education :** Vladimir enters Šiauliai gymnasium (and not Russian Cadet Corps as expected for a member of his class).

1875 **Expo :** The first agricultural exposition is initiated in Šiauliai by Nikolajus Zubov. He has built a flour mill, a plant manufacturing farming tools, and a beer brewery.

1875 **Shelter :** His mother Aleksandra opens a shelter for seniors and a shelter for orphans and the disabled.

1876 **Stipends :** Nikolajus gives stipends to students in Šiauliai gymnasium.

1880 **Education :** Sofia attends the prestigious Bestuževo school, in St. Petersburg, the only higher school for women in the Russian Empire. She is the first Lithuanian woman to enroll in higher education.

Vladimir studies science at St. Petersburg University, through 1886.

1884 **Marriage :** August 6th. SBZ marries Count Vladimir Zubov, whom she meets while he is at St. Petersburg University. (She is 24 and he is 22.)

They maintain close ties with the socialist party "Proletariat" youth. Their closest friends from that time are exiled to Siberia. The goal of the patriots was to give up their property and titles, go underground and devote themselves to a revolutionary fight against the Tsarist regime.

1886 **Education :** Vladimir graduates from St. Petersburg University in chemistry. While a student, he joins the Lithuanian and Polish Socialist Party and is an officer on the party committee. He forms a group supporting war refugees. Starts a newspaper "New Lithuania."

1887 **More Study :** With her husband, SBZ studies at University of Halle in Germany. He studies veterinary medicine.

1887 **Son born :** Their son Vladimir (1887-1959) (the second Vladimir) is born while they are in Halle, Germany. (SBZ is 27.)

1888 **Withdrawal :** Vladimir Zubov formally leaves the Proletariat group.

1890 **Electricity :** Under Nikolajus, electricity is connected to the Ginkūnai estate.

1890 **Move :** They settle in Šiauliai first, and then Ginkūnai. They build a new manor house, and VZ engages in animal husbandry, applying knowledge he'd gained in Germany. (SBZ is 30.)

1891 **Daughter born :** Daughter Aleksandrą (1891-1961) is born.

1894 **Charity org :** Nikolajus supports a charity Žiburėlis that helps poor children attend school.

1896 **School :** Senior Zubovs found Lithuanian schools for workers at all five estates, paying the teachers' salaries. The first school, at that time a secret, is in the basement of Ginkunai manor. Then Naisiu, Gubernijos, Dabikines, and Medemrodė. They are officially Russian schools but they secretly teach Lithuanian language, which is illegal.

1896 **Agric work :** The first dairy is started in Ginkūnai. There is also a seed research bed, cattle breeding experiments, horse, sheep and pig breeding. Butter sold under the brand.

Vladimir actively supports the Lithuanian nationalist movement. He founds and distributes a newspaper.

1898   **School :** The manor house in Šiauliai is donated to become a high school for girls: Didizdvario Gymnasium.

1899   **"Festival"** : June 12th, a "folk festival" is held as cover for people planning a nationalist movement. Others are held, e.g. 1904.

1900   **Library :** The Zubovs found the Public Library Society and donate books and acquire books from publishers in St. Petersburg. The library is transported to Russia later, to save it, and it is looted, and lost.

1902   **Novel & Book :** Sofia publishes her novel in Polish. Her husband destroys all printed copies but misses one.

Her father Hipolitas Bilivicius publishes "Thoughts About God, or the human condition," in Polish.

1904   **"Festival"** : June 12. There is a large gathering in Kairiai as another "folk festival." About 300 actors, priests, students. While attendees watch a play, there is a political meeting to discuss how to deal with the Tsarist government. These types of meetings lead to the organization that becomes the Lithuanian Democratic Party.

1903-   **Pogroms :** Pogroms lead to mass Jewish emigration.
1906

1905   **Worker strikes :** There is a general strike among factory workers that leads to armed rebellion. Fights between Cossacks and workers break out. The Russia Empire is destabilized.

1905   **Ban lifted :** The Russian ban on a Lithuanian press and language is lifted.

1905   **Schools :** Schools are now taught in Lithuanian exclusively. Sofia inspects schools for quality and herself teaches science and often gives public lectures for adults.

1905 **Romance?** : Vaclovas Bielskio (1870-1936), the brother of socialist Jono Bielskio, arrives with his Ukrainian wife, Verą Ušakovą (1877-1941) and two daughters, to be a teacher for Vladimir.

In 1906 he becomes the administrator of Aleksandra Zubovienė's estate, thus his family is close to the Ginkūnai family.

1907 **Publishing** : Vladimir takes over a newspaper. Supports the Literature, Drama and Music Society.

1908 **Son marries** : Son Vladimir marries Ona Jakubauskaitė (1885-1975) while still a student, before earning a doctorate in 1910. He lives on the Dabikinės estate.

1909 **Grandson born** : Son Vladimir has a son also named Vladimir (1909-2007).

1909 **Separation?** : The elder Vladimir and Sofija choose to live separately. He moves to Medemrode, about 12 kilometers from Ginkūnai.

1910 **Ag school** : Vladimir's mother Aleksandra (mother-in-law to SBZ) founds a program in animal husbandry and dairy farming in Bubiai. Her son Dimitri later continues the work.

1910 **Love child** : A child is born out of wedlock, fathered by VZ. He is 48 at the time, the maid is 23. VZ provides a house (near north of Ginkūnai), a "pseudo house-husband," and financial support to mother and daughter. The child is one year younger than his first grandchild.

1911 **Grandchild** : Son Vladimir has a second child: Ona Zubovaitė-Ortelienė (1911-1979).

1911 **Divorce :** The couple divorce after 26 years of marriage. (ages 51 and 49) Sofia stays in Ginkūnai with the household of her daughter Aleksandra and her husband Jonas Fledžinskas.

His assets are divided three ways, for himself, his son and his daughter. (SBZ declines a share.)

1913 **Death of elder :** Vladimir's mother Aleksandra (SBZ's mother-in-law) dies on September 14, 1913. She is buried in a cemetery in Bubiai.

1914 **WW I :** Germany declares war on Russia.

1914 **War disruption :** Vladimir helps hide a man who escapes from Siberian exile. During First World War, many Lithuanians are forced to flee to St. Petersburg. SBZ, her daughter Aleksandra and Jonas Fledzinskas flee the approaching war to Moscow and then Crimea.

1914 **Seminary :** The Zubovs house a teacher's seminary in their manor in Didžiadvare. A new building is postponed due to the war.

1915 **Daughter marries :** Aleksandra marries Jonas Fledžinskas in Crimea, where they are waiting out the war.

1915 **Army service :** Son Vladimir is commissioned into the army. He invites Jonas Fledzinskas to join him as an administrator (the latter was excused from military service because he was an only surviving son in a family). This protects him from the draft, in case the rule excusing him was reversed.

1915 **Lith. Language :** J. Fledžinskas reunites with his wife and her mother in Moscow. They begin learning the Lithuanian language. When they return to Ginkunai they begin to speak the language at home.

1916   **Newspaper :** Vladimir founds New Lithuania newspaper. His articles call for Lithuanians to get ready to go back to their estates.

1917   **Grandchild :** Son Vladimir has his third child, Marija Zubovaitė-Dementjevienė (1917-1986)

1918   **Tsar murdered :** Tsar Nicholas and his family are killed.

1918   **Independence :** February 16th. Lithuanian Independence Act. Versailles Treaty.

1918   **Return :** SBZ, her daughter and son-in-law return to Šiauliai and live in Didžiadvarė temporarily because the Ginkūnai manor is in ruins.

1919   **Grandchild :** Grandchild Vytautas Fledžinskas is born to Aleksandrą.

1920   **Grandchild :** Granddaughter Sofija Fledžinskaitė (called Zulė) is born to Aleksandrą. Sofija BZ is much involved with the children.

1922   **Seminary :** Parkland around Didžiadvare is donated and the manor is sold to the Education Ministry and becomes a Pedagogic Institute, later the Art Faculty of Šiauliai University. Also, the Ziburelis Society, a cultural organization, and consumer cooperatives.

1923   **Grandchild :** Granddaughter Aleksandrą Fledžinskaitė (called Alė) is born to daughter Aleksandrą (called Alina).

1924   **Grandchild :** Grandson Jurgis Fledžinskas is born to daughter Aleksandra.

1926   **Official visit :** The President of Lithuania visits Ginkūnai.

1929   **Assoc formed :** Aleksandra Fledžinskeinė and her mother found an association called "Ginkūnai Estate."

1929   **Birthday :** Sofija's 70th birthday is a grand celebration, with tributes written up in the press.

1932   **Death :** June 9th. Sofija dies in Kaunas at the age of 72. She is buried near Ginkūnai.

1933   **School :** The primary school in Ginkunai is named after Sofia and Vladimir Zubov.

1933   **Death :** Vladimir dies June 23 in Medemrode at age of 71.

1940   **Soviets occupy :** June 15th, first Soviet occupation

1940   **Retreat, flight :** The Ginkūnai estate is nationalized and designated a Soviet cooperative. The Fledzinskas family moves to Skaudvile, Jonas' original home, to lead a simple life. They and their son Jurgis who remains in the country are saved from deportation to Siberia by a family friend with connections. (The other Fledzinskas children and their spouses flee the country and become refugees, finally settling in the USA and in Australia.)

The second Vladimir Zubov? (son of the first Vladimir) was deported, and Jonas Fledzinskas paid the Russians to let him return to Lithuania.

1941   **Deportation :** Vladimir's second wife Vera is deported to Siberia and dies in exile, at 64 years old.

1941   **Nazis occupy :** June 22nd, Nazi German occupation

1944   **Soviets occupy :** July. Second Soviet occupation, through 1991.

1959   **Memoir :** Son-in-law Jonas Fledžinskas finishes his memoir in Skaudvile.

1959 **Son passes:** Vladimir Zubov (the second one) dies at age 72.

1961 **Daughter passes** : Daughter Aleksandra Fledzinskienė dies in Skaudvile at age 70.

1965 **Son-in-law passes** : March 1st. Jonas Fledžinskas dies in Skaudvile at age 80. He is buried there.

1985 **Museum** : A small museum is established in the primary school on the Ginkūnai estate.

1991 **Free Lithuania** : February 16th, independence, after 47 years of Soviet occupation.

Broader Context, Turn of the 20th Century

By Ruta Sevo

An Early

History of

Shifting Status

The current geographic area that constitutes Lithuania has gone through many phases of ethnic and political dominance.

At the end of the 14th Century, the majority of the population was East Slavs, who, facing aggression from Moscow, turned to the Poles for protection. At that time, Lithuania geographically included all of Belarus and Ukraine. The official language was Old Byelorussian, not Lithuanian.

The Lithuanian language was spoken by peasants, who constituted about 75% of the population and who mainly spoke Lithuanian. Polish gentry (landowners) made up about 10%, and ethnic Germans and Jews made up about 15%. Townspeople were mostly Jews, Germans, and Polish/Lithuanian gentry. Polish became the language of the upper classes, who saw themselves as both Poles and Lithuanians.

For over two centuries, Lithuania and Poland were a shared state, ruled by Polish and Lithuanian nobility. The Polish language became the dominant language among all the nobility, although Lithuanian nobles retained their cultural identity. In Western Lithuania (Samogitia) they never ceased to speak Lithuanian.

Many of the Lithuanian state's nobles remained Orthodox, although others converted to Christianity, eventually to Catholicism. The two religions (East and West) competed throughout the period.

The University of Vilnius was founded in 1579 and became a preeminent educational center for eastern and central Europe. Vilnius was a capital on the border between Western and Easter Christianity, and considered "the Jerusalem of the North" among Jews. It became a major cultural center.

Various wars and plagues decimated 40% of the population. The nobles fell out into competing factions. In 1795, the state collapsed and the Russian Empire took over 90% of the territory.

A long period of Polish domination ended in the late 18ᵗʰ Century, when Poland itself was partitioned, and the Russians became rulers of the entire region except the southwestern part of Lithuania taken over by Prussia.

In this new Russian province, the Russians banned the name "Lithuania," imposed the use of the Cyrillic alphabet, and limited economic development. Schooling in Polish survived until 1863.

After an uprising in November 1830, Tsar Nicholas I began an intensive program of Russification and closed the University of Vilnius.

Serfdom was abolished in the entire Russian Empire in 1861.

By 1897 there were 2.7 million people under the Russians. About 87% lived in rural areas, 13% in towns. Peasants comprised 73% of the population, townsfolk 20%, and nobles 5%. Languages: 58% Lithuanian, 13% Jewish, 10% Poles, 15% Eastern Slavic.

Clearly there were distinct cultural and linguistic communities living side by side.

Many townspeople were necessarily multi-lingual. There were at least 350 shtetls, or Jewish settlements, spread throughout the region.

National
identity

The idea of a Lithuanian nation was advanced among intellectuals in the mid-19th Century, with heavy focus on the roots of the language.

In 1864, the Lithuanian language was banned in schools. There was a prohibition against printing and a press. There were attempts to dismiss the language as lacking in prestige.

Russians attacked Catholic churches. However, the ban on the press was lifted and thousands of books were published. The language was standardized, with a grammar published in 1901.

An uprising in 1864 failed to break ties with Empire. Lithuanians pulled away from Poles. Schools were being de-Polonized and Lithuanian university students were sent to St. Petersburg or Moscow instead of Warsaw.

Emigration
1867-1868

A massive famine drove over 600,000 people (20% of the population) to leave.

The countryside was underdeveloped by European standards.

Pogroms[71]

1881 to 1884 and

1903-1906

One wave of anti-Jewish aggression came after Jews were blamed for the assassination of Tsar Alexander II.

A much bloodier wave of pogroms broke out from 1903 to 1906, leaving an estimated 2,000 Jews dead and many more wounded.

The pogroms led to mass Jewish emigration. Two million Jews fled the Russian Empire between 1880 and 1914, many to the United States and United Kingdom. It precipitated the rise of Zionism among Russian Jews.

Records show that there were at least 350 shtetls, or Jewish settlements, spread throughout Lithuania when the Nazis invaded, and a population of 200-250,000. Their populations had little interaction with others except that they dominated in markets and commerce. They had independent schools in Hebrew.

---

[71]https://en.wikipedia.org/wiki/Anti-Jewish_pogroms_in_the_Russian_Empire

Uprising 1905	Uprisings of workers and peasants in 1905 led to the Tsar's concessions, such as schooling and a press in Lithuanian and new Catholic churches.
Russo-Japanese War 1904-1905	Plans to expand the Russian Empire lead to war in the Far East, in competition for Korea and Manchuria. Many men are conscripted to fight and very likely die. Many choose to flee and emigrate instead.
1918	The Romanov dynasty came to an end. Tsar Nicholas II and his family were killed.[72]
World War I	During World War I, the Germans gained a stronghold in the area and occupied it for three years. Vilnius fell to the Germans.
Independence 1918-1940	After the War, in February 1918, Lithuanian leaders declared the country independent. Russian efforts to reclaim the territory failed; they recognized independent Lithuania in 1920. Vilnius was named the capital, but Poles seized the city in 1920. The Lithuanian capital was moved to Kaunas.

---

[72] See http://history1900s.about.com/od/1910s/fl/Murders-of-Czar-Nicholas-II-of-Russia-and-His-Family.htm

There was increasing polarization and competition between ethnic populations living in towns. There were those speaking Polish (24%), Lithuanian (8%), and Belarussian (22%). The large Jewish population (42%) spoke Yiddish or Russian.

Less than 3% of the population of Vilnius spoke Lithuanian. It was the language of peasants and farmers -- 93% of Lithuanian-speakers were peasants; only 4% of townsfolk and 2.5% nobles. In Kaunas district, up to 6.7% of the nobles were Lithuanian-speaking.

Among Polish speakers – 41% were peasants, 30% nobles, and 26% townsfolk.

Independence
1920-1940

Following World War I, an independent Lithuania started to rebuild its infrastructure. Land reforms starting in the 1920s shifted ownership from the estate holders to the state and to cooperatives.

Nobles took a low profile, due to the threats of persecution after the Russian revolution and its distain for elite classes. To some extent the dominance of Poles among gentry contributed to the notion that the gentry were a foreign-born ruling class and landlords. Many participated in nation-building but had to overcome a history of privilege and power in the countryside.

For 19 years, Kaunas was the temporary capital of Lithuania while the Vilnius region was under Polish rule.

About 28% of those who were nobles by birth and lived in the region spoke Lithuanian. The percentage of nobles speaking Lithuanian in Kaunas administrative district (the capital of Independent Lithuania) was higher: 36.6%. The majority of nobles -- 59% -- spoke Polish, so the association of nobility and Polish heritage was strong.

During this period, a complete educational system was developed. The city of Kaunas gained a university and developed other urban characteristics, serving as the capital.

Until 1940, economy was primarily agricultural – dairy farms and livestock. There were few natural resources, mostly peat and amber.

The period saw the rise of Lithuanian nationalism.

World War II
Russian
Occupation
1939-1942

At the start of World War II, in 1939, Germany and the Soviet Union divided up Eastern Europe, and they assigned Lithuania to Russian dominion. The Russians overthrew the independent

Lithuanian ruling regime and governed it as a republic starting in 1940. Between 1940 and 1941, the Soviets deported thousands of Polish-Lithuanians to Siberia.

German Occupation 1942-1944

In 1941, the Germans invaded and pushed the Russians out. With possible cooperation from locals, they massacred the Jewish population of 240,000 (10% of the total population), as well as Polish intelligentsia.

Russian Occupation 1944 & 1945

The Soviet army returned in 1944 and 1945. The Russians deported 150,000 individuals to Siberia – anyone considered educated, elite, or a leader , including teachers, religious figures (of any denomination), and government workers.

Vilnius as a city was altered irrevocably. The Vilna ghetto holds the memory of extreme ethnic oppression and genocide. Many remaining Poles relocated to Poland in 1946. The Lithuanian language was allowed in schools and newspapers continued to be published in the Lithuanian language.

Russification took hold. The Soviets collectivized agriculture and pushed industrialization, moving more people into cities, including migrants from Soviet areas. By the 1960s, native Lithuanians started to enter the system as Communist leaders.

Around 1988, Gorbachev introduced a program of reform that encouraged local control and decentralization of satellite countries called Perestroika.

His action encouraged the formation of Sajudis – the Lithuanian Movement for Perestroika. Sajudis campaigned for complete independence, beyond decentralization. The Lithuanian Community Party declared independence in December of 1989. The Sajudis-led parliament declared an independent Lithuanian state in January of 1991.

Independence
1991-

To solidify its independence, Lithuania joined NATO in November of 2002 and became a member of the European Union in 2004.

In 2001, 67.2% of the population lived in cities and 33% in rural areas. Up until WWII, most of population had been farmers and peasants.

For ethnic composition, in 2001, Lithuanians were 83% of the population, Russians 6%, and Poles 7%. There were pockets of Belarussians, Ukrainians, Tatars, Karaites, and 3,000 Romani (who survived German extermination). (Karaites are a branch of Judaism, with 250 members located mostly in Vilnius and Trakai. They speak a Turkish-based language using the Hebrew alphabet.)

In terms of religion, in 2001, 79% of the population is Roman Catholic.

Others: Russian Orthodox 4%; Jews 4,000; Lutheran 20,000; Evangelical Reformed 7,000; Sunni Muslim 2,700.

Language

Sanskrit and Lithuanian are closely related linguistically, with roots in the Indo-European language transported by the Aryans to India. Lithuanian and Latvian are the oldest Indo-European languages still spoken, and have a grammar as complex as classical Greek.

Nobility[73]

The Polish-Lithuanian Commonwealth (16th-18th Century) had one of the largest percentages of nobility in Europe, close to 10% of the population, in some regions, like Samogitia, it was closer to 12%.

With Polonization and Russification over centuries, identities mixed culture, language, and geographic area of birth. For example, nobles in Lithuania could identify as Lithuanian and speak Polish at home, or originate from Polish genealogical lines. They intermarried with

---

[73] https://en.wikipedia.org/wiki/Lithuanian_nobility

French, Italian, and Russian as well as Polish nobles.

In independent Lithuanian between the wars, the government of Lithuania issued land reform limiting manors with 150 hectares of land, while confiscating land from those nobles who were fighting alongside the Polish in the Polish-Lithuanian War. Many members of the Lithuanian nobility during the interbellum and after the World War II emigrated to Poland, and many were deported to Siberia during the years 1945–53 of Soviet occupation.

Darwinism and
Social
Darwinism

Sofija Zubov's novel references Darwin's theories a number of times.

Charles Darwin (1809-1882) was an English naturalist who states that all species of organisms arise and evolve through the natural selection of small variations, or adaptations, that increase the ability of an individual to compete, survive, and reproduce, and assure the survival of his species.[74]

---

[74] https://en.wikipedia.org/wiki/Darwinism

Since SBZ studied natural sciences in St. Petersburg, she likely encountered Darwin's ideas as they were spreading through universities.

His ideas informed what is called Social Darwinism – the application of the principle of the struggle for survival to society, and usually in support of the idea that philanthropy is counter-productive, because it tries to remedy the conditions of "weaker" members of society.

SBZ has a dialog on this very question in her novel. She was clearly preoccupied with his theories and interpreted them for her personal philosophy of life: that the family construct was essential for raising children, that it assured their survival in society, among other things.

There were many derivative ideologies that could be seen as mis-appropriations of Darwinism in later years. Still, late in the 19th Century, his ideas reached and lit intellectual fires in St. Petersburg.

Photo Album

Sofija Bilevičiūtė-Zubovienė 1860-1932
This photo is displayed in schools founded by the Zubovs

Vladimir Zubov 1862-1933 (about 1932)

Sofija Zuboviene, Vytautas, Aleksandra, Sofija

Sofija Bileviciute-Zuboviene with four grandchildren
ca. 1924

SOFIJA BILEVIČIŪTĖ-ZUBOVIENĖ, IPOLITO ŽMONA
(1860.V.27—1932.VI.9)

Aleksandra Zubovaitė ir
Sofija Bilevičiūtė - Zubovienė. Apie 1909

Best view of Ginkunai estate, concrete balcony added

Ginkunas school museum, artifacts from estate

Gruss aus Schaulen

Weekly market in Siauliai

Šiauliai. Sodo gatvė.

Šiauliai. Sodo street

Šiauliai, Vilniaus g-vė.

Šiauliai. Vilniaus street

260

Made in the USA
Middletown, DE
31 May 2017